THE UNEXPECTED MARQUESS

SUZANNA MEDEIROS

THE UNEXPECTED MARQUESS

A new Marquess, a chance meeting, and a hidden identity…

He was simply John Evans when he enlisted ten years ago. But when John returns to England after the war against Napoleon is over, he gains an unexpected title —the Marquess of Lowenbrock.

Niece to the former marquess, bluestocking Amelia Weston pretends to be a barmaid for one night as research for the novel she's writing. When one of the tavern's patrons tries to take liberties, a handsome stranger comes to her rescue. Days later, Amelia is shocked to discover the new marquess is none other than the stranger she met all too briefly that night. The same man upon whom she's based the hero of her novel. Unsure about his reaction to her recent adventure, she must now hide her identity even as she finds herself drawn to him.

When John inherited a title and an estate, no one told him he'd also be responsible for the shy Miss Weston. But he can't help growing closer to this woman who reminds him, at the most inconvenient times, of the voluptuous barmaid he met during his last night in London.

To learn about Suzanna Medeiros's future books, you can sign up for her newsletter at https://www.suzannamedeiros.com/newsletter.

CHAPTER 1

April 1816

J OHN EVANS WAS ON THE WAY to becoming well and truly foxed. His mouth was beginning to take on an unpleasant taste, and a warm buzz had settled over his senses. At this rate, he'd be in no condition to set out for Yorkshire tomorrow. His vision was still clear, however, so he ignored his normal caution.

This was his last evening in London, not that he'd miss the place. He longed for the quiet country life of his youth. But he would miss the two men sitting at the table with him now, laughing as they shared some of the pleasant memories they'd experienced over the past few years. They were the brothers he'd never had. No one wanted to talk about the friends they'd lost during the long war with Napoleon, not tonight, but they'd never be forgotten.

"And then Sir Galahad decided to jump in and rescue the poor damsel!"

Baron Cranston slapped John on the shoulder, the wide grin on his face indicating he was equally deep in his cups. "How have I never heard this story before?"

The Viscount Ashford grinned. He raised his cup in a mock salute and downed the rest of the liquid. "I was saving it. Since this will be our last evening together for the foreseeable future, I figured there was no point letting it go to waste."

John crossed his arms and scowled at Ashford. His friend never tired of tormenting him about John's inclination to jump in without thinking when a woman needed assistance.

"I have two sisters, as you both know. If you sorry lot were similarly afflicted, you'd understand what it is to feel the need to come to a woman's rescue."

Ashford shook his head. "I do have sisters, so that excuse doesn't apply. No one here would stand by and allow a woman to be taken advantage of. But we draw the line at saving light-skirts from plying their trade."

Another round of raucous laughter accompanied that statement, and somehow John kept from punching his good friend.

Their carefree mood was contagious, and he found himself struggling not to laugh with them. But it wasn't a laughing matter, especially since it was true. After failing to stop his older sister from sacrificing herself in an unwanted marriage to save their family, he'd developed the inconvenient inclination to rush in whenever he saw a woman in jeopardy. Sometimes before he'd even taken full stock of the situation.

And as it turned out, Louisa's marriage was a happy one. From what he'd seen of her and the Marquess of Overlea during his current stay at their London town house, it was clear that they were very much in love with one another.

He downed the rest of his drink and forced his thoughts away from the angry youth he'd been when he discovered his sister was about to wed the head of the family that had ruined theirs. There was no point in allowing the ale to go to waste, but he wouldn't order another.

"Evans."

He met Ashford's gaze, and the man inclined his head to the scene that was taking place at the back of the tavern. "What say you? Genuine dismay or yet another game to entice more coin from the man in question?"

John's eyes narrowed as he took in the scene. He wasn't surprised to find the woman in question was the dark-haired beauty he'd been trying to ignore all evening. He scowled at the rowdy group of men who were giving the barmaid a difficult time. Her attempts to escape the hands that were reaching for her lacked the arch coyness they all knew meant she wasn't trying to escape.

"It doesn't look like a game," Cranston said.

All eyes turned to John as his longtime brothers in arms waited to see what he'd do.

"The devil take you both." John rose to his feet, working to keep his growing anger under control. Anger that wasn't aimed at his friends. He knew both men would step in to help the woman, but for some reason they took an inordinate amount of pleasure in watching him do so.

Like the horrible cliché of a knight coming to the rescue of a fair damsel, John strode to the back of the room where one of the men had succeeded in drawing the unwilling woman onto his lap.

Having learned his lesson from previous attempts to save women who were engaging in a bit of play to up the price for their wares, he didn't rush to attack. Instead, he stopped right before the man who was so intent on holding on to the woman in question that he didn't notice John's arrival.

His gaze collided with that of the woman, and what he saw in her deep blue eyes told him he'd been correct in his original assessment. Her pupils were dilated with unmistakable fear, her breathing shallow. He'd seen those signs on the faces of many men often enough during battle. He held his hand out to her and waited. Without hesitation, she grasped it and allowed him to pull her to her feet. In one swift movement, he placed himself between the woman and the rowdy group that had now become silent.

It took the woman's assailant a moment to realize what had happened. When he stumbled to his feet, John was relieved to find they were of equal height. But he didn't relax his guard. They were in an unsavory part of London, so it was almost a guarantee the man would have experience brawling. Fortunately, John had learned a few things himself during his years of military service, and this man didn't intimidate him at all. Ashford and Cranston were watching and, if necessary, would jump in to lend their assistance.

The man swayed slightly and clenched his hands into fists. "Now see 'ere, there's no reason to argue. Go on your way, and we'll forget this 'appened."

John didn't even try to hide the loathing he felt for the man, who'd been attempting to force himself on an unwilling woman. The heat of his scowl was enough to give the other man pause.

John turned to look at the woman. Her fear was clear to see, and he didn't need to ask what she wanted him to do.

Still, she shook her head and mouthed the words "Help me."

He turned back to the group, all of whom were now standing. There were five of them to the three in John's own group, but these men hadn't just come back from war. John had no doubt that if it came down to a fight, he and his friends would come out the victors.

They were saved the effort, however, when another barmaid joined them.

"I'll be taking over your table, gentlemen. Molly is needed in the kitchen." Her words were punctuated with a heavy hint of innuendo as she leaned forward to place a tray of drinks on the table. Her bosom threatened to spill out of the top of her dress, which had the immediate benefit of capturing the attention of the other four men at the table. But the lout who'd been intent on claiming his original prize hesitated, unwilling to give up the battle. Fortunately, all it took was a wink from the new barmaid and her hand on his arm to capture his complete attention, and his eyes focused on her ample cleavage.

John turned to face the woman whose name he now knew was Molly. She intrigued him more than he cared to admit, having captured his attention from the moment he'd stepped into the tavern earlier that evening with his two companions. She must have been new to her position, for she lacked the experience dealing with customers that the second barmaid clearly possessed. She was shaking, her breath coming in short, rapid pants and her pupils blown wide. From her extreme reaction, it was clear she'd never had to deal with unwanted advances before tonight. At least not from men who were willing to take first without asking permission.

He started to reach for her elbow, wanting to lead her away, but thought better of touching her. In that moment she wouldn't welcome even an innocent touch from a man. Instead, he clasped his hands behind his back. "I can escort you to the kitchen to ensure no one else bothers you. You'll be able to find a moment of peace there."

She took a shallow, unsteady breath and looked away. When her gaze met his again, she gave her head a sharp shake. "I need to leave."

He followed the direction of her gaze and saw that the owner of the tavern, a portly middle-aged man who'd been very welcoming to him and his friends when they'd first arrived, was making his way toward them. From the stern expression on the man's face, John assumed he was about to take the woman beside him to task for being less than welcoming to the lout who'd wanted more from her than someone to serve him drinks.

The path to the front door of the establishment would bring them face-to-face with the owner. "Is there an exit to the back? Perhaps off the kitchens?"

Nodding, she turned and headed away. He hesitated, unsure if he should follow. She stopped after a few steps and looked at him. Time stood still as he became aware yet again of just how bewitching this woman was. Her dark hair was pinned up with several loose tendrils escaping its haphazard arrangement. He could see that her eyes were a deep shade of blue he'd never seen before, and her generous lips, one of which was clenched between her teeth, had his thoughts wandering down unwelcome paths.

He'd already noticed her figure in the tight serving outfit that all the other barmaids wore. But her neckline was more modest, a scrap of pale white linen tucked into her décolletage to hide the bounty that lay beneath. When he'd first noticed it—because he'd been unable to stop himself from taking in her figure when she'd caught his attention—he'd assumed she wore it as a way to differentiate herself from the other women, to draw out the curiosity of the men she served. But now it was clear to him that she wasn't used to the attention she'd gained and had tucked in the scrap of fabric to preserve her modesty.

She glanced past him again, and her eyes widened when she saw that her employer was almost upon them. She crooked her finger at him in invitation. He followed, a quick glance telling him that the tavern owner had stopped his pursuit, a small smile of satisfaction on his face. It was obvious he assumed Molly was leading him somewhere private for a tryst.

Instead of leading him to the kitchens, she slid behind a dark curtain that, to his surprise, hid a doorway. For a moment he wondered if he'd misread the situation entirely, but nevertheless, he followed when she slipped through the opening.

They were in a dimly lit hallway, but the woman didn't stop as she made her way down its long length.

She struggled for a moment with the bolt on the final door but finally managed to pull it back and escape through it. Catching a glimpse of a dark alley, he followed. He hadn't saved her just to have her fall into mischief outside. It was very late and the streets—especially an alley—wouldn't be safe.

He'd almost have to follow as she fled down the alley. Instead, she stood with her back to the dirty tavern wall, her eyes closed as she took in deep breaths of air. He kept his distance so as not to alarm her.

A full minute passed before she opened her eyes and met his gaze. "I cannot express how grateful I am to you for your assistance."

Her accent reminded him of a fellow soldier he'd once known who'd claimed to be from the north of England. A million questions sprang to mind, but he restrained his curiosity.

He accepted her thanks with a bow of his head. "It was the very least I could do." He waited a beat before asking the one question uppermost in his mind. "Are you certain you should be working here? Not that I'm judging you, heaven knows there are worse fates that can befall a woman. But you seemed to be out of your depth."

She released her breath with a soft sigh. "It was my first night. I've never done this type of work before."

"Are you planning to return?"

He could see her wrestling with the answer. Finally her shoulders slumped. "No, I think it best that I don't. Alice was able to distract that patron once. There's no telling what could happen the next time."

His sense of relief was immediate. He didn't know this woman, but he felt an odd sense of protectiveness toward her.

"Are you returning inside?" She seemed to realize the double meaning behind her question, for she rushed to add, "I'm not issuing an invitation. I was merely curious."

He found himself staring into Molly's face for several long moments, drawn to her more than was wise. "My friends are still inside, and it will be the last time I see them for some time."

She gave her head a sharp nod. "Of course. I should be off then."

She turned to walk away, but he couldn't allow her to disappear into the night unprotected.

"I'll walk with you to the main street. I have a carriage waiting for me. It can take you home and then return for me later."

Her smile was shaky, but it had the effect of making him feel as though he were ten feet tall.

Without another word, they made their way down the dark alley. When they finally reached the street beyond, the scant lighting from the waning moon offering very little light, John was glad he'd been there to help this woman. The second barmaid—Alice, the woman next to him had called her—might have succeeded in diverting the lout's attention without his assistance. But the thought of this woman, who only came up to his shoulders, trying to make her way home alone in the dead of night left him with a sense of dread.

The alley had led them to the end of the street, and it was another full minute before they reached the front of the tavern. He'd caught the attention of his coachman when they were still several buildings away. By the time they reached the tavern's entrance, the carriage was rolling to a stop next to them.

"You won't be returning to work here?" He'd already asked the question, but he had to make sure.

When she met his gaze, her expression was impossible to read, and for a moment he feared the worst. Finally she sighed and shook her head. "I think it best I give up the silly notion of working in a tavern."

Her statement struck him as odd. A young woman taking up such a line of work in a part of town that was less than savory wouldn't normally refer to the pursuit as a *silly notion*. Normally it was an act of necessity.

He wanted to ask so many questions. Her full name, for one, and where she lived. And if he could see her again. But of course he remained silent. He would be leaving London on the morrow after he met with his solicitor. There would be no time to get to know this mysterious woman who had captured his attention so thoroughly.

After telling the coachman that he was to take the young woman home and then return, John took a step back as she gave the man her address. The street name meant nothing to him—he hadn't been in London all that long.

After helping her into the conveyance and closing the door behind her, he watched in silence as the coachman flicked the reins. The smile she bestowed on him through the window as the carriage pulled away had him wishing he could rearrange his plans for the rest of the evening.

When he rejoined his friends, they wasted no time in provoking him.

Ashford raised his glass in a toast. "Here's to another damsel saved."

Cranston raised his own glass in salute. "It won't be the same when you're buried up in Yorkshire. Who will be left to save all the pretty young women in London?"

John snorted. "The two of you will have to pick up the slack. Unless you'll be heading home as well?"

"Perish the thought," Cranston said with an exaggerated shudder. "I may have given up my commission, but I'm in no hurry to rejoin the family."

Ashford merely shook his head. They'd all heard his stories about how Ashford's father had encouraged him, his heir, to enlist with the hope that he would die and the title would pass to his younger brother. "Will you be taking up your seat next year?"

John barely resisted the urge to reach for the new drink that had appeared during his absence. He might not see his friends again until then, when he would be ready to take up his new position in the House of Lords. Thinking about his current rise in social status made him more than a little uncomfortable. "I don't know. That will depend on what I find when I reach the estate in Yorkshire. I didn't even know we were related to the Marquess of Lowenbrock, no matter how remotely. I certainly never expected to inherit. But with my luck, the estate will be crumbling and I'll be drowning in debt."

"You haven't spoken to the solicitor yet?" Cranston shook his head. "You need to do that before you leave."

John scowled, remembering the daily notes the man had sent his way since he'd arrived in London two weeks ago. "I'll have to. I'm not even sure where the estate is. He left me one last note telling me that unless he hears otherwise, he'll be at the house tomorrow morning."

With a scowl, he reached for the drink his friends had ordered for him. He no longer cared about the hangover he'd be suffering the next day. Nor did he want to remember the woman he'd never see again.

CHAPTER 2

ORMALLY AMELIA WESTON WAS UP WITH THE SUN, but she'd gone to bed later than normal the night before. Which meant she'd only just fallen asleep when her maid woke her with news that Mr. Markham needed to speak with her as soon as possible. So instead of sleeping the morning away as she'd hoped, she found herself seated at the breakfast table at her normal hour.

The kind stranger's carriage had deposited her at the town house after midnight just as Mr. Markham's coachman was preparing to make its own trip to pick her up from the tavern. She'd been planning to wait in the shadows until its arrival but had jumped at the man's offer. After the rough treatment she'd experienced, she hadn't wanted to risk someone else with ill intent coming across her while she was outside alone.

After arriving safely at her family solicitor's town

house, she'd spent several hours making notes about everything she'd experienced that night at the tavern. That included every detail she could remember about the fair-haired hero who'd rescued her.

She'd been at the tavern to conduct research for her new book after she'd failed to sell her first novel. The criticism that it was clearly written by someone who'd led a sheltered life had struck home.

So she'd made the journey to London, determined to experience the outside world firsthand. She'd known it would be dangerous, but she'd never expected someone would be so free with her person as to pull her onto his lap. She wasn't certain Alice—the barmaid she'd paid to aid her should the need arise— would have been able to save her if that stranger hadn't stepped in and drawn her out of harm's way.

It had taken most of the carriage ride home for Amelia's shock to subside. When it finally did, her mind had begun to whirl with ideas for her new book.

Her second novel would not be dismissed as boring. No, this book would be about a young woman whose family had fallen on hard times and who'd found herself forced to work in a tavern to help them. Her imagination had stalled after that initial premise, hence her decision to set foot in a tavern herself and experience everything that took place within its walls.

Now she knew her heroine would be saved by the hero of the story. Being stubborn and independent, characteristics she possessed herself in no small measure, her heroine would resist the pull of attraction. But instead of merely arranging for her safe return home, as the gentleman who'd assisted her the evening before had done, the hero of her story would see her home himself.

Nothing untoward would happen, of course. It would hardly be heroic for him to force himself on her after saving her from another's unwanted attention. But he'd insist on seeing her again. And when her heroine refused, given the difference in their stations, he would appear the next evening at the tavern—her guardian angel—to watch over her.

"Miss Weston, did you hear what I said?"

Amelia let out a soft sigh and met the gaze of the elderly gentleman who sat across from her at the breakfast table. Mr. Markham, her family's solicitor, had been kind enough to allow her to stay with him for the past week since she had no other family or friends in London. He'd always acted like a kindly uncle to her, especially during the past three years while they'd waited for the new owner of her uncle's estate to return to England.

Her smile was sheepish. "I'm afraid I was woolgathering."

Mr. Markham's mouth twisted in a slight frown. "I said that you need to return to Yorkshire. Today."

Amelia sat up straighter, thoughts of the stranger who'd helped her uppermost in her mind. Of course she hadn't planned on returning to the tavern, not after her narrow escape the night before. But despite the fact she knew it was unlikely, given the number of people in town, she'd hoped to run into him somewhere else.

"Why so soon? Has an urgent matter arisen at the estate?"

The solicitor met her gaze head-on. "The new marquess has finally replied to my letters and informs me that he plans to visit the estate as soon as possible. He'd planned to call on me at my office later this morning in fact. I cannot emphasize how important it is that you be in residence at Brock Manor when he arrives. He'll never believe you have nowhere else to go if he learns you are in London and might not allow you to continue living at the estate."

She gave her head a shake. It couldn't be... It was too soon. She had to find her gallant savior. "But—"

"Today. It may already be too late. He plans to quit London as soon as possible. I'm going to have to delay him for at least another day if you're to arrive in Yorkshire before him."

Disappointment settled over her, but ever practical, Amelia pushed the emotion aside. There would be no fairy-tale endings for her. Not that she'd expected it in the first place. But it seemed her brief adventure in town had come to an end.

"I'm sorry." His voice was soft, sympathy shining from his pale blue eyes. "But we both know this is for the best. Perhaps you can visit another time, once your position at Brock Manor is secure."

She stretched her hand out across the table. He did the same and engulfed her hand in his, giving it a quick squeeze before releasing it again.

"Will I see you before I leave?"

He shook his head. "I've taken the liberty of asking the staff to begin packing your belongings. When I finally meet the elusive new marquess, you should already be on your way home."

"Of course." She swallowed her disappointment. Clearly the Fates hadn't changed their minds about her lot in life. But her dreams would live on in her novel. Her heroine would have the fairy-tale ending that wasn't meant for Amelia.

CHAPTER 3

*L*EAVING TOWN WAS MORE DIFFICULT than John had imagined, and not because of the headache that he normally suffered after a night spent drinking. No, the problem had been Mr. Markham, the ancient solicitor to the Lowenbrock marquisate.

John had first learned of his change in status three years ago, while away fighting Napoleon. Time might have passed, but he found it impossible to believe he was now a lord. A marquess, no less. The irony was striking. He'd left England without a penny to his name, relying on an old family friend to help him secure a position in the British army. And now he was a member of the landed gentry.

He'd come to terms a long time ago with the sacrifice the older of his two sisters had made when she'd decided to wed the head of the family that had ruined theirs. It hadn't mattered to him when he was only eighteen that the Marquess of Overlea hadn't been involved in the events that had led to their family living in poverty.

Louisa had sent him several letters, attempting to reassure him she was happy in her marriage, but she couldn't be trusted to be entirely truthful with him. She'd always tried to shelter him and Catherine. But his younger sister had never glossed over facts, and Catherine had insisted Louisa and Overlea were in love.

John had seen for himself that the man treated her with affection and catered to her in almost all things. It had shocked John to see the once-aloof stranger he'd met only briefly before the marriage now content to show a softer side of his personality before others, but he'd soon come to realize that Catherine's reassurances were true. Overlea loved his sister.

He'd worried when news had arrived that Catherine had wed the following year. A friend of Overlea's whom John had met after Louisa's wedding. The man had seemed nice enough, but Catherine was still so young, and he feared for her happiness. He'd been content to be proven wrong in that matter as well.

Ten years had passed since he left England, but it might have been a lifetime. Overlea had done what he, John, had been unable to do when their family tottered on the brink of complete ruin. He'd swept in and saved Louisa and Catherine, setting the stage for their future happiness. And he'd wanted to save John too, promising to fulfill John's dream of attending Oxford.

John had given up that dream when he'd enlisted and now found himself a lord in his own right and no longer reliant on the charity of others.

The stage was set for his own salvation. A future he'd never imagined for himself. But of course, it hadn't been as simple as meeting with the Lowenbrock solicitor and setting off that day for his new estate. What he'd thought would be a straightforward meeting with Markham had turned out to be a complicated ordeal that had delayed his departure for two days. The solicitor had paperwork he insisted John had to sign before leaving for Yorkshire. Given that the elderly man had tracked him down almost three years ago and requested he return to London to assume his new responsibilities, it was baffling that all the documents hadn't already been prepared. Perhaps the forgetfulness that came with old age was finally taking hold of the man. He was at least sixty years of age, though John wouldn't be surprised to learn he was approaching his seventies.

Of course, his sisters had been ecstatic to hear he'd be in town a little bit longer. He was staying with Louisa and Overlea, but Catherine and her husband, the Earl of Kerrick, seemed to have made the town house their second home. And with his nieces and nephews, the place was bedlam. He kept waiting for some indication that his brother-in-law was annoyed by the constant noise, but the man seemed to revel in family life.

This time John wouldn't be leaving in the dead of night. No, this time the entire family was present to see him off. It was the third morning after he'd said goodbye to his friends and, good or ill, he was anxious to see what his new future would hold.

Louisa drew him into a tight hug that would have had him squirming when he was younger. But he would miss her as well, and he returned the embrace with abandon.

She finally drew back after what must have been a full minute. Unshed tears brimmed in her gray eyes as she clutched his hands. "You haven't been here long enough to make up for all the years you've been gone."

He gave her hands a squeeze before releasing them. "Well, I'm in England to stay now. When things are settled at the estate, I'll invite you all. We'll get sick of each other soon enough then."

Catherine gave him a fond smile. "Never." Her head tilted to one side, and she lowered her voice. "I've missed you. After that last argument we had before you left... Well, I'm glad you survived your time fighting Napoleon. I can't even begin to imagine what you've been through."

Louisa frowned at the reminder of how he'd escaped into the night on the day of her wedding. "Disappear like that again and I'll come after you myself."

A stab of well-deserved guilt speared through him. The anger he'd felt toward his eldest sister all those years ago had long since disappeared. He knew mere words could never make up for the hurt he'd caused her, but he needed to say them. "I owe you an apology for how I treated you all those years ago. My behavior was selfish. I should have spoken to you first before leaving."

Louisa reached for his hand, almost as though she were afraid to let go. "It was a stressful time. Papa had just passed away, and we were struggling to stay afloat."

He took a deep breath before replying, holding back the anger that threatened to surface. "Catherine told me about Edward Manning's proposition and why you had to go to Overlea for help."

Louisa's face twisted into a slight grimace. "I hoped you'd never learn the truth."

"Why, because you thought me young and foolish enough to challenge him to a duel? If that was your fear, it was a valid one. I would have done exactly that and probably gotten myself killed."

"Instead, you ran off and put yourself in even more danger." She was quiet for a few seconds before continuing. "I wanted Nicholas to go after you. To use whatever connections he had to bring you home."

He wasn't surprised by the revelation. He'd been more surprised that she hadn't done just that. "What changed your mind?"

"Honestly? He did. I was so angry with him, then disappointed, but he was right. You were a young man who needed to find himself, and it was time for me to stop treating you like a wayward child. No good would have come from attempting to drag you home. But I couldn't stop myself from worrying about you. I'm so glad you've finally returned."

"You needn't concern yourself with worries about my running away again. Ten years in the army was more than enough. Of course, I'm sure there is adventure to be had in the colonies…" Somehow he held back his smile as a frown settled between Louisa's brows.

Louisa swatted him on the shoulder, and he laughed, relief flooding him at seeing her smile.

Louisa's husband approached and held out his hand. John clasped it in a firm handshake.

"Thank you for looking after my sisters when I wasn't able to." There was a lump in his throat, but he spoke around it.

"Your sister has brought me more happiness than I'd imagined possible. But please, take care of yourself. And write often. It will be difficult for her to let go."

Catherine laughed. Her husband, the Earl of Kerrick, placed an arm around her shoulders, and she looked up at him with a fond smile. Another happy marriage, thank the heavens.

"Don't worry," Kerrick said. "With the children around and getting into all sorts of mischief, your sisters have more than enough on their minds. You needn't worry they'll lock you in a room to keep you from leaving again."

Louisa's eyes lit at the suggestion. "Now that you mention it…"

John gave her another hug. "A locked door might have held me back when I was a youth, but now it would be child's play to escape."

Louisa's smile wavered, and he cursed himself for the casual reference to all he'd undergone while away at war. She had asked him about his experiences, but not wanting to worry her, he'd glossed over the many horrors he'd seen. Her smile brightened again after a moment, and he had to give her credit for not pursuing the subject. The sister he'd once known would have hounded him for all the details.

The horses snorted behind him, his cue that he should be on his way. He'd dreaded coming home again, imagining he would be smothered by Louisa and, to a lesser extent, Catherine. But he'd enjoyed this family reunion. Becoming friends with Overlea had been an unexpected benefit. And Kerrick… Well, it was impossible not to like the man. He had a sense of humor that never failed to chase away John's darkest memories.

"I must be going now. I have a long ride ahead of me."

Catherine embraced him again, then Louisa. Their smiles when they stepped back were as different as the two women. His younger sister's grin was bright, hopeful. She'd always seen the best in people and in most situations. Louisa's was genuine, but there was a hint of sadness hidden behind it.

"I promise to write, although I hope my letters will be lacking in excitement. I'm looking forward to settling into a quiet life in the country. And perhaps you'll be able to visit soon."

"We'll hold you to that," Catherine said.

A footman opened the carriage door for him when he turned. He gave the man a curt nod of thanks as he climbed into the conveyance, a traveling coach that apparently now belonged to him given it sported the Lowenbrock crest on the door.

John settled back against the cushions, refusing to look out the window. There was only so much emotion he could handle, and he refused to allow this departure to be a melancholy one. He'd meant what he'd said when he promised he'd be seeing his sisters again soon. With any luck, the house he'd inherited would be livable. His solicitor had also assured him that he was a wealthy man.

And as he'd had to remind himself several times

since first learning of his inheritance, he was now a marquess. He wasn't sure he'd ever adjust to that fact.

The carriage glided over the cobbled streets with very little jostling. He'd never traveled in such luxury before, but he meant to make use of the time ahead. A leather portfolio waited for him on the seat opposite. Markham had insisted he needed to read the documents it contained, but John had yet to even glance at them. He couldn't put it off any longer. It was time for him to become familiar with what it meant to be the Marquess of Lowenbrock.

With a slight smile, he pulled out the first of several large envelopes and scanned through the contents to gain a quick overview of the documents. The carriage ride would take two days if he stopped for the night. He wouldn't be able to make his way through all the documents if he read through them with care, but he would have a good head start.

He hadn't expected to find enjoyment in the task. Until that moment, he hadn't allowed himself to think about how much he'd missed his studies. His father hadn't been able to afford a tutor for him, but he'd studied all manner of subjects with the help of their parish's reverend. Granted, he'd been studying classical languages, familiarizing himself with works of literature and gaining a modicum of proficiency in any subject Reverend Harnick had introduced. John's greatest wish had been to procure one of the scholarships to Oxford that were made available to those who showed promise but who wouldn't otherwise be able to attend.

He'd long ago come to terms with the death of that dream. After all, facing down a field of enemies who wanted nothing more than to see you dead had taught him to focus on the present. On killing without taking in the faces of the men he ran through with a sword.

Against all odds, his life had returned to what it had once been, only better. Never again would he have to fight daily for his very life. He had a new challenge ahead of him in figuring out what it was that lords did all day other than go to their clubs. And he no longer had to worry about his sisters.

Of their own accord, his thoughts drifted back to that night at the tavern, when he'd said goodbye to his brothers in arms. His second family. But instead of thinking about when he'd see Ashford and Cranston again, he couldn't help but remember the woman he'd saved. Molly.

He'd gone back to the tavern last night, making an excuse to his sisters that he wouldn't be out long. And he'd meant to keep that promise even if Molly had been there. But true to her word, he hadn't spotted her. He'd been relieved and had sent up a silent prayer that she'd be able to find another occupation that was safer. Taking in sewing perhaps. Louisa had done that to bring in extra money before she married Overlea.

But another part of him had been disappointed he wouldn't see her again. Her creamy, fair skin had served to make her eyes stand out. Were they as deep a blue as he remembered, or had his mind embellished that detail? It had been dark in the tavern, and there hadn't been any lamps outside when he'd escorted her to the carriage, so he couldn't be certain. Her dark hair had started coming undone, and he thought about what it would have felt like to remove the hairpins and allow the mass to fall. How far down her back would it reach?

He was jerked from his thoughts when the carriage came to a halt and the door was thrown open moments later.

"Has something happened?" he called out.

The carriage would have jostled slightly if the coachman had descended from his seat, so he thought to see one of the outriders who were accompanying the coach. The last person he expected was the frail form of his solicitor being helped into the carriage by one of those outriders.

A quick glance out the window told him that they'd stopped before the man's office. John was struck speechless. He hadn't expected to see Markham again. The solicitor certainly hadn't mentioned he'd made arrangements for the coach to stop by his office before John quit London.

Markham thanked the man who'd helped him

into the carriage and settled onto the seat opposite John, next to the portfolio of paperwork.

"It's a good day for a journey, is it not?"

The slight twinkle in the man's eyes told John he wouldn't like what was coming next. When the carriage began moving forward again, dread settled in the pit of his stomach. Still, he hoped for the best.

"Was there something you forgot to mention yesterday? I'm sure you could have sent me a letter. And where are we taking you?"

Markham's smile widened, the action telling John what was happening before the words were spoken. "I'm going with you to Yorkshire, of course."

John barely contained his groan. The man never stopped talking. Would he have any time to even glance at the papers he'd intended to study during the journey?

John's eyes narrowed. "Is that necessary? I thought you worked for me now, and I certainly don't recall asking you to accompany me today."

Markham made an attempt to school his expression, but John couldn't miss the amusement reflected in his eyes. "I'm being paid handsomely to see to your needs, and there is no better way to ensure you settle in without any issues than to come along and offer my assistance."

John wanted to insist otherwise, but a grimace of pain on the older man's face forestalled his complaint.

"These old bones aren't used to travel, even in a

carriage as well appointed as this one. Perhaps it would help if we switched seats and I faced forward?"

John gave up since it was clear the man wouldn't be dissuaded. He moved to the bench opposite and then offered his assistance to Markham, who made quite a show of wincing as he rose from the seat and shifted to the more desirable location John had just quit.

It took the man far longer than it should to settle in before meeting John's questioning gaze again.

Markham leaned forward and gave him a quick pat on the knee. "Worry not. I'm sure the hours will speed by now that you have company."

CHAPTER 4

*T*IME DID NOT SPEED BY.

John had planned to stop at posting inns along the route to arrange for fresh horses so he could arrive in Yorkshire as quickly as possible. If the coachman was still alert, he'd hoped to make the trip in one day. He wouldn't overwork the man, but he'd ensure everyone accompanying him on the trip was well compensated for their extra effort.

But after the first hour of travel, during which they'd barely left the outskirts of London, he had to revise that plan when Markham made it clear that he had no intention of staying in the carriage that long. The man insisted on stopping at every inn they passed to stretch his legs and relieve himself—something he'd assured John would happen to him as well when he got older. John said nothing, merely sitting in the carriage and waiting for the solicitor's return. His patience threatened to snap, however, when he heard Markham instruct the coachman to moderate the speed at which they were traveling. Apparently every small bump in the road caused the man's bones to ache.

John grit his teeth and said nothing when his solicitor was helped into the carriage after yet another break. He hadn't realized that England possessed so many inns, but after their third stop in as many hours, he began to wonder if Markham had an ulterior motive for delaying John's arrival at Brock Manor.

He considered and discarded a myriad of reasons for such a delay between the man's many monologues and attempts to draw John into conversation. After all, his solicitor had been aware of his arrival in London for some time now. The many letters and requests for meetings he'd received bore witness to that fact. If Markham had wanted to delay John's departure from London, he wouldn't have done everything in his power to arrange a meeting as soon as possible.

Which left John with a mystery, for he was almost certain Markham was hiding something. Only time would tell if it had something to do with the estate. John wondered if he would have been able to solve that mystery if Markham stopped talking long enough to give him the opportunity to look through the documents with which he'd insisted John familiarize himself.

When the sun began to set, John welcomed the

upcoming reprieve. He'd already come to terms with the fact they wouldn't be traveling through the night. Markham would never survive such a long journey.

When they exited the carriage to partake their evening meal, John informed the coachman that they'd be staying at the inn for the night.

Markham clapped him on the back. "I hope I haven't delayed you too much. I know it must be a trial, but I appreciate the consideration you've shown." He nodded toward the taproom. "I'll meet you there in a moment after I secure rooms for the night."

John didn't argue. If there was one thing he needed after the tortuously slow journey, it was a drink.

CHAPTER 5

*I*T WAS BOTH A BLESSING AND A CURSE that Amelia's bedroom window faced the front of Brock Manor. On the one hand, it allowed her to keep a vigilant eye on the tree-lined avenue visitors would take to reach the house. That meant she wouldn't be caught unaware when the new marquess arrived. But it also meant she found it next to impossible to think about anything else.

She'd long since given up even attempting to get any writing done that day. She hadn't fared better with the book she was in the middle of reading and so had taken up some needlework. There was something about the rote activity that soothed her when her nerves were on edge or when she was having difficulty with her writing.

Her chair was positioned next to the wide window,

the heavy draperies drawn back to let in the midafternoon sun. She kept glancing out the window to see if a carriage approached, but at least she was making progress on what would soon be a cushion. That was in stark contrast to how her writing was going.

She blamed her lack of inspiration on her uncertain future. She couldn't help worrying about what would happen when the new marquess arrived. Would he be young or old? Mr. Markham hadn't shared any information with her, and truthfully, she hadn't asked. All she'd known was that the man was away from England and either unwilling or unable to return. Since her uncle's death three years ago, she'd fallen into the routine of her days—broken only by her recent all-too-short trip to London—and had ceased to think about the man.

But since hastily departing London, she couldn't concentrate on anything else. Would the man be content to ignore her, allowing her life to continue as it had been before his arrival? Or would he insist on marrying her off to someone, anyone, to get her off his hands? If the latter proved to be his intention, perhaps she'd be able to convince him to give her a small allowance that would allow her to move into a small cottage of her own. She wasn't against the idea of marriage, but she wouldn't be pushed into a union with someone she barely knew. At the age of five and twenty, she was old enough to refuse any such attempt. But the fact she was now well past the age of majority meant little if the man decided to tie up the funds the previous marquess had set aside for her dowry.

For what felt like the millionth time that day, she glanced up from the square of fabric that was destined to be a chair cushion and looked out the window. Expecting to be disappointed yet again, she glanced down automatically at her embroidery before registering the fact that a carriage had turned onto the avenue that led up to the house.

The effect of that realization was immediate. Her heart began to race and her hands became unsteady. She set aside the needlework and watched the approaching carriage. It moved at a steady pace, the Lowenbrock crest emblazoned on the door of the gleaming black traveling coach announcing that the new marquess had arrived.

Amelia rose and moved closer to the window, hoping to catch a glimpse of the man when he exited the carriage.

Of course, that meant he might also be able to see her. She moved to one side of the window so the drapes would hide her if he happened to glance up. She'd decided he was likely a man of middle age. Had he been in the Americas all this time? That would be why it had taken Mr. Markham such a long time to find him. But that begged the question—was he in England to stay?

She resisted the urge to press her nose against the

pane of glass, but it was a near thing when she saw Mr. Markham exit the carriage. He hadn't mentioned during that last breakfast in London that he planned to accompany the marquess.

Her gaze remained fixed on the carriage door. She saw his hand first, gloved of course. Then one broad shoulder and a fair head of hair. Her breath caught. Something about the man reminded her so much of the one who'd come to her rescue that night at the tavern.

It couldn't be him. Life wasn't like that. It would be too large a coincidence to think she'd be caught out in the only adventure of her hitherto placid life by the man who held complete control of her future.

She told herself it was nothing more than a superficial resemblance. England was filled with men who had fair hair after all. Still, she held her breath when he raised his head to take in his new home.

Her heart threatened to stop. For a moment she wondered if she would give in to the trite cliché of swooning, because the man who'd exited the carriage *was* the same man she'd seen at the tavern.

His eyes passed over her window, and she realized she'd stepped closer to it when his gaze hesitated before he turned to ask Mr. Markham a question.

Had he seen her? Did he recognize her?

She stepped back and turned away. He couldn't recognize her. He couldn't know she'd been pretending to be a barmaid as research for a novel. She cringed at the thought.

She recalled that her hair had been looser than how she normally wore it, scraped back into a chignon. That had been Alice's doing. She'd allowed Amelia to tuck a kerchief into the neckline of the dress she'd had to don for her role as barmaid, but then Alice had taken the liberty of removing several hairpins and threading her fingers through her hair to loosen the thick mass. Several strands had even escaped.

Quickly she moved to her chest of drawers and searched through the top one. It had been a while since she'd worn a lace cap to cover her hair, but she knew there must be several in there still. Much as she hated the things, she hadn't wanted to give them away lest the new marquess be old-fashioned enough to expect her to wear one.

Well, he wasn't old-fashioned—at least she didn't think he was since he was of an age with her. She sighed with relief when she found the neatly folded stack of white fabric tucked into the back of the drawer.

She reached for the top one and moved to her dressing table. Her hands were still shaking as she smoothed the cap over her hair, careful to ensure no strands escaped. She examined her appearance in the mirror.

Ugh, she looked like someone's maidenly aunt, but she supposed that was a good thing. Would he recognize her? The world was filled with dark-haired, blue-eyed women. A few days had passed, and it had been dark that night. Surely he wouldn't recognize her and realize they'd already met.

Her spectacles. She didn't really need them most of the time, but they did help if she was working by candlelight. Her eyes became fatigued otherwise.

She opened the middle drawer of the dressing table, pulled out her one pair of spectacles, and put them on. Normally she left them perched on the end of her nose, hating how they dulled her vision when she was looking into the distance. With firm resolve, she pushed the spectacles up and glanced at her reflection. She had to lean closer to get a good look.

Would he be fooled? If he'd taken in her too-wide mouth and her nose, which turned up a bit at the end, he might recognize her. But men weren't usually that observant. The former marquess hadn't been. If he ran into someone he should know where he didn't expect to see them, he behaved as though he were meeting that person for the first time.

The spring fair in the nearby village had been filled with such occurrences. Amelia had taken to leaning in and whispering someone's name to her uncle whenever they approached. He acted gruff whenever she did so, as though annoyed with her assumption he wouldn't recognize the person, but she knew he'd appreciated her service.

Sadness swept through her as she remembered how kind he'd been when she first came to live with him. Her parents had died when she was still far too young, taken from her by a virulent fever that had swept through the household. She'd been saved when they sent her away to school after one of their staff died, but her parents hadn't been able to avoid the illness and had also succumbed to it.

Her uncle's own wife had passed away the year before during childbirth, and he'd never wed again. From the moment she arrived, he'd treated her like the child he never had. He'd been gone for three years, but she still missed him.

She moved to her bed and lowered herself onto the edge. Mrs. Brambles, a gray tabby, slept soundly in the middle of her bed. There was a perfectly good cushion for her on the floor by the window, but she ignored it most days in favor of Amelia's larger bed.

Amelia stroked the cat's head. Mrs. Brambles squinted, one amber-colored eye opening slightly. She closed it again and turned onto her side with a contented purr.

Amelia smiled. "You'll have to be a good girl for me. No escaping when the maid comes in later. We don't know yet how the new marquess feels about cats. It's possible he might take one look at you and consign you to sleeping in the stables."

The tabby made a small sound of protest and curled into a tight ball.

"Yes, I wish I could go to sleep as well and put off this meeting."

She stood and began to pace. Her spectacles had slipped to their customary perch on the tip of her nose, but she ignored them. She only needed to push them up when she was around the new Marquess of Lowenbrock after all.

Lowenbrock. The man who'd saved her from ruin at the tavern. The man after whom she'd decided to model the hero of her current novel. Well, this had the potential of being awkward.

He must never know about her writing. If he read any of it, he'd realize who she was. And then he might kick her out into the cold. Mr. Markham would take her in, of course, but she couldn't impose on him forever. He lived in bachelor's quarters, and they were constantly in one another's pockets when he returned home from his office.

She glanced at the small clock on her bedside table. Only ten minutes had passed since the carriage pulled up in front of the estate. What would be happening downstairs? She knew the staff would have gathered in the front hall to greet the new marquess.

The house had been a flurry of activity since her return, when she'd informed them of his impending arrival. Not that the house wasn't normally well kept, but there had been bedrooms that hadn't been dusted

46

for some time. Mrs. Hastings and her husband, the head housekeeper and butler, had marshaled the staff, even calling in extra help from the village, to clean the house from top to bottom. Amelia had stayed in her room for most of that time, not wanting to interrupt the many people wandering through the house.

Everything had been declared ready the night before, and the staff had been on high alert, as had she, for the arrival.

She smoothed her hand over the light yellow muslin dress she wore. It was of simple design with tiny sprigs of white flowers dotted throughout and had a modest neckline. It was a far call from the tight, low-cut dress she'd borrowed during her research stint at the tavern. That dress had been made for a much smaller woman and had clung to her curves indecently. Below the swell of her bosom, the fabric of her dress fell in a smooth, straight line that concealed her generous hips. This time when the blond stranger looked at her, he'd see nothing but the very respectable Amelia Weston, niece and ward of the former Marquess of Lowenbrock. With any luck, the new marquess would have already forgotten the barmaid he'd met a few nights ago.

She wondered how long she'd have to wait before being called downstairs. Would Hastings take the marquess on a tour of the house, or would Mr. Markham suggest they call her down first? She could wander downstairs on her own. This was her home, after all, and it would be customary for her to greet him.

She gave her head a small shake. Mr. Markham had definite plans about how their introduction would go, and she would follow his lead in this matter.

CHAPTER 6

*A*FTER SUFFERING THROUGH the uncomfortable task of being presented to the staff, John wanted nothing more than to escape. He'd thought himself prepared, but being presented to Hastings, the butler, and the rest of the staff hadn't seemed real.

It seemed that Markham referring to him by his title and his friends subjecting him to many warnings about the changes in store for him now that he was part of the aristocracy hadn't been enough to prepare him for that moment. To his sisters, he'd still been their brother John, and that was how he still thought of himself. He was older and he'd seen much death in the years since leaving England, but he still thought of himself as the same person he'd always been. His brothers-in-law had tried to call him Lowenbrock, but John had insisted they use his given name. They'd complied because they were family.

But to the alarmingly large number of servants arrayed neatly in two long rows in the spacious entrance to his new manor, he would only be known as the Marquess of Lowenbrock and addressed as "my lord."

All those eyes on him, deferential yet curious, served to underscore just how different his life was from the genteel poverty of his youth. Life as the son of an impoverished, untitled gentleman was no preparation for the future he now faced, the lives of the tenants for whom he was responsible.

And he still had to get through the documents Markham had kept him from studying during their two days of travel together. Then he'd have to meet with the estate's steward.

With the ruthless efficiency born of many years at war, he forced his thoughts away from everything he needed to do and concentrated, instead, on trying to remember as many names as possible. He noticed that the head housekeeper was Mrs. Hastings, leading him to the assumption she and the butler were married.

He'd never been comfortable speaking before large groups, so when the introductions were over and it became apparent they were all waiting for him to say something, he shot an exasperated look at his solicitor. After spending the past two days talking off John's ear, surely the man could have warned him. He managed a few words, thankful when Markham gave him an approving nod when he was finished.

He jumped at Markham's suggestion they partake of some refreshments before being taken on a tour of the house and followed the man into the drawing room.

John collapsed into a blue wing chair that was clearly meant more for entertaining than for comfort. For a moment after dropping into it, he feared it would collapse. But the piece was sturdier than he'd expected and held his weight.

He tipped his head back and closed his eyes, not caring that he could feel the solicitor's eyes on him.

"You can just command everyone to leave you alone for the rest of the day. Even me."

John opened one eye before closing it again. "I didn't think anything could get you to stop talking."

Markham gave an amused harrumph. "I suppose I deserve that."

John opened his eyes and watched the old man settle into the chair opposite. A fire had been lit, and the warm tendrils of air reached out to comfort him. "I know I'll adapt in time, but deuced if this isn't uncomfortable for me. It feels like my first days after enlisting all over again. I fast learned just how soft and sheltered I'd been up to then."

"One step at a time, my lord. This estate has been running without your guidance for several years now. It will continue to do so while you become acquainted with your position."

John let out a breath of air. "I suppose there's

some comfort in that. But for now I plan to enjoy a proper cup of tea and whatever small sandwiches the cook has prepared. I only hope she made a fair amount, because I'm famished."

Markham examined him intently for a moment, leaving him to wonder what he'd said that would elicit such scrutiny.

Finally the man gave his head a small shake. "You can just ask for more if there isn't enough. The staff is unfamiliar with you, but they will adapt if you let them know what you like."

John tried to ignore the small twinge of awkwardness at the reminder that everyone under the manor roof existed to serve him. How long would it take for him to stop feeling like a guest in his own home?

Markham continued to scrutinize him, and John had the uncomfortable feeling that he was about to impart unwelcome news.

"Out with it, Markham. There's no point in keeping secrets now."

"Of course, my lord." He seemed to consider his words for a moment, and John waited, his alarm growing with each passing second. "There might be one matter I neglected to mention."

Here it was. John was going to learn that the surprisingly large amount of money he'd been told he now possessed was spoken for and that the former marquess owed a rather large fortune as a result. Debts John would be required to pay.

He braced himself for the bad news. It was what he'd expected, after all, when he'd learned he'd inherited a marquisate.

"The former marquess, may he rest in peace, had a niece. One with whom he was quite close."

Those were not the words he'd been expecting. "You already mentioned that his wife died in childbirth and that he didn't have any children. I'm glad to hear he wasn't entirely without family."

"I'm happy you feel that way, because I need to inform you she is in residence here."

For a moment he didn't know what to say. Why would Markham keep this from him? He must have worried John would cast the woman out. It occurred to him she might be a child. "How old is his niece?"

"Five and twenty. In the years since the marquess's death, she has been running the estate with the advice of the steward."

Markham didn't mention the fact he'd first reached out to John's family three years ago and that it had taken him so long to return to England. He also did an admirable job of concealing any censure he might have felt about John's absence.

"Was she told about me?"

Markham nodded. "Yes. She knows you're expected and is no doubt waiting to meet you."

"She's not married?"

"Alas, no. Her uncle arranged for her to have a

season but then he fell ill. He lingered for several years, and she wouldn't hear of leaving his side."

John couldn't help but think about his eldest sister, who was the same age when she wed. "And now she is past the age when society would deem her acceptable." He wasn't able to keep the note of rebuke from his tone.

Markham sighed, and the way his mouth turned down told John he wasn't pleased. "Just so."

John shrugged. "Then we shouldn't keep her waiting. She can join us for refreshments, and we'll become acquainted."

A footman entered then, and John smiled as he examined the trolley that was wheeled into the room. Tea and sandwiches instead of sweets. Good. The sandwiches were small but there were a great deal of them.

He waited as the man removed the trays from the trolley and placed them on the low table before the settee.

"Williams is it?" John asked the young man when he was finished. When he nodded, John thanked him. It wasn't strictly required, but he hoped never to become one of those people who took the serving classes for granted. "Could you also ask if Miss—" He looked at Markham when he realized the solicitor hadn't given him the young woman's name.

"Amelia Weston."

John nodded. "Could you ask if Miss Weston is available to join us?"

The footman replied with an "Of course, my lord" and turned to fulfill his request.

John shook his head after he'd left the room. "I'm not sure I'll ever become accustomed to that."

Markham gave him a piercing look that had John feeling as though his insides were exposed. He couldn't help but wonder if the solicitor found him lacking. After all, why else would Markham have altered his plans and decided to accompany him to Yorkshire? Either he didn't think John was up to the task ahead or... It only just occurred to him that he might be concerned for Miss Weston. That must be the reason for Markham's last-minute change of plans.

John allowed his thoughts to drift to his friends as he and Markham waited. He couldn't help but imagine what Ashford and Cranston would say when they learned he was now responsible for a woman only two years younger than him. They'd tease him mercilessly about how it was a fitting duty for him. Which of course led him to thoughts of the woman he'd helped in the tavern that last night he'd seen them.

It took a great deal of effort to wrench his thoughts away from her.

Markham was quiet, which was out of character for the man.

The sound of soft footsteps approaching had them rising to stand.

When she stepped into the room, it was almost impossible to tell what she looked like. She wore spectacles, and her hair was covered with a lace cap. Her figure, of course, was hidden by a loose gown, yellow in color, that only showed she was slim. He couldn't help but notice the generous swell of her breasts, but aside from that, the fabric flowed straight down from the bodice. Overall, her appearance was that of a woman who didn't want to draw attention to herself.

She stepped farther into the room, her gaze averted, and waited for Markham to make the introductions. John could see she had a pale oval of a face. Not one strand of hair was visible, but from the dark sweep of her brows over the spectacles she wore, he knew her hair would be dark.

Markham smiled at the woman, genuine warmth in his expression. "Miss Weston, may I present to you the Marquess of Lowenbrock?" He turned to John. "My lord, I have the great pleasure of introducing Miss Amelia Weston."

The woman in question still hadn't met his gaze. John bowed his head in greeting while Amelia gave him a deep curtsy. When she straightened, her eyes finally met his, and he experienced a sharp jolt of recognition. Which left him unsettled because he couldn't place how he knew her. He wouldn't have run into her on the continent, not if she'd been living here and helping to run the estate. So why did he feel as though they'd met before?

"It is an unexpected pleasure to meet you, Miss Weston."

Her smile was restrained, but still it caused a strange sense of warmth to go through him. Her glasses had slipped down her nose and their eyes met again before she glanced away and pushed them back up. But in that moment he'd seen they were the same bright blue as the barmaid he'd met several nights ago. Molly.

But this woman was nothing like the barmaid. Molly had worn a dress that had accentuated her lush curves. She'd been free in her speech and had seemed comfortable in his presence. Miss Weston, however, was modest in both dress and demeanor. And the way she held herself, every muscle almost tense aside from the nervous fiddling of her fingers, which she clasped together at her waist, told him a great deal about her feelings. She was either frightened of him or nervous about her future in this household.

Well, he wasn't about to cast her out. That fate had befallen his own family, and his sister had found it necessary to marry a stranger to save them all. It had turned out well in the end for Louisa and Catherine, but everything in him balked at the idea of behaving in such a villainous manner.

An awkward silence had settled over the room, and John found himself wondering why Markham

57

wasn't trying to break it. Heaven knew the man was capable of prattling on incessantly.

A streak of gray fur caught his attention, and he watched as a slim cat approached Amelia and rubbed against her legs.

"And who is this?" he asked.

CHAPTER 7

SHE'D BEEN IN A STATE OF ANXIETY since
she'd spotted the new marquess. But in that
moment her greatest fear was for the cat who'd
streaked past her when she exited her bedroom.

Her uncle hadn't been a fan of felines, claiming
they caused his eyes to water. Sometimes when they'd
been near the mousers that were kept in the stables,
she'd witnessed him sneezing with an alarming
amount of force. On one occasion, she'd feared he
wouldn't be able to catch his breath, so it was no
wonder her uncle had denied her request to bring one
of the kittens into the house.

She'd only acquired a kitten after he'd passed
away. What if this man was similarly afflicted? She
didn't think she'd be able to give up Mrs. Brambles,
who'd been her constant companion these past three
years.

Lowenbrock tilted his head when she didn't answer him right away. Wonderful—now he'd think her a lackwit.

She took a steadying breath. "Mrs. Brambles," she said. But she found herself unable to leave it at that. "Please don't make me send her to the stables. I promise to do a better job keeping her in my room. You won't even know she's here."

Lowenbrock's brows drew together and she held her breath, expecting the worst.

"I don't have an issue with cats. She might not be too happy if I decide to get a dog or two, but of course she can stay."

She froze in place when he crouched and held out a hand, making a soft clicking sound with his teeth.

The cat looked up at her, and Amelia felt compelled to explain the cat's reticence. "She doesn't go to strangers unless you bribe her with... food."

She watched, stunned, as the cat moved from her side to examine Lowenbrock's fist. When he opened his hand, she sniffed it to see if it contained anything edible. But then, instead of stalking off when she found it empty, she allowed him to stroke her under the chin. When Mrs. Brambles tilted her head back to signal he should continue, Amelia realized her mouth was gaping. She closed it with a snap.

"She's never done that before. She's usually cautious around people she doesn't know."

He looked up at her from his crouched position,

his boyish smile telegraphing his pleasure with the recent turn of events. "I've been told I have a way with animals."

And with women, no doubt, she thought.

He gave her a curious look, and for one horrible moment, she thought she'd spoken aloud. But if that was the case, he said nothing as he rose. Mrs. Brambles returned to Amelia's side as if to tell her she hadn't abandoned her owner. She rubbed against Amelia's legs and then sat, her curiosity about this stranger evident in the way she kept her gaze focused on him.

"Is there a story behind her name?" Lowenbrock asked.

Amelia nodded. "She was fearless as a kitten. Unlike her littermates, who were content to remain in the stables near their mother, she liked to explore. She wandered as far as the house one day, her fur matted with tiny brambles from her travels through the gardens. When I tried to return her, the kitten followed me out of the stables again. She was old enough to be separated from her mother, and so I brought her home with me." She reached down to give the cat an affectionate scratch beneath one ear. "She's not to be trusted around fish."

Lowenbrock laughed, the sound a low rumble. "I'll keep that in mind."

Amelia looked away, uncomfortable with the

weight of this man's attention. Her gaze settled on the tea tray and refreshments.

"I'm sure you and Mr. Markham are famished, my lord. We should enjoy the tea while it is still hot."

"A woman after my own heart," Mr. Markham said.

Amelia shot him a fond smile, glad for his presence, and moved to the settee. This introduction would have been difficult for her if he weren't there, but there was something about the older man's presence that served to comfort her. After her uncle passed away, Mr. Markham had made it a point to visit often. At first it was to help her with the running of the estate, but later she knew he came to visit with her. She might have lost her uncle by blood, but in the intervening years she'd gained an honorary one.

Lowenbrock informed her that he took his tea without milk or sugar. She poured a cup and handed it to him, careful to ensure their hands wouldn't touch. When she noticed that the man's hands were bare, she regretted not taking a moment to don her gloves before leaving her room. Something about the thought of him taking her hand, as he'd done when he'd helped her up from that other man's lap at the tavern, had a flood of heat going through her. She refused to examine why and turned to prepare cups for Mr. Markham and herself.

Mr. Markham did an admirable job of filling in the moments of silence, and so she sat primly, nibbling on the edge of a sandwich while she watched the new marquess swallow one whole. He noticed her regard, and his expression turned sheepish.

She turned to Mr. Markham when he asked her a question, silently berating herself for being caught staring, and pushed her spectacles higher on her nose. If she wasn't more careful around the new marquess, he'd realize they'd already met.

When the plate of sandwiches was finished, Lowenbrock rose from his chair. "I'll take my leave now. Markham here has left me with a great deal of paperwork, and I've scarce glanced at it. It was a pleasure to meet you, Miss Weston."

She inclined her head by way of response.

"Markham," Lowenbrock said. "I'll see you at dinner. If I have any questions…"

Mr. Markham nodded. "Of course. We'll see you then."

Amelia waited until the marquess had left the room before turning to the solicitor. She whispered, "We must speak privately."

CHAPTER 8

*M*ARKHAM RAISED ONE HAND to indicate Amelia should remain quiet. After several seconds passed, he walked to the doorway and glanced out into the hallway. He saw the butler leading Lowenbrock to the back of the house where the marquess's study was located. Lowenbrock might have put off the house tour, but Markham knew he would have to submit to it before dinner.

Satisfied they were safe from being overheard, he returned to his seat. He'd noticed the strange way Lowenbrock had looked at Amelia. It had also been obvious the marquess made her nervous. She was normally composed among strangers, and he'd never seen her appear so meek.

Markham had always been fond of Amelia, and after her uncle's passing, they'd grown closer. She had no other male relative in the world to look after her, and so he'd stepped into that role. He needed to get to the bottom of the strange tension that existed between the two before he returned to London.

It was Amelia who spoke first, her voice soft. "You didn't tell me you planned to accompany His Lordship."

Markham shrugged. "It was a last-minute decision. I had to delay him en route since he hoped to travel through the night. I needed to ensure you had sufficient time to settle in after your trip."

Amelia tilted her head. "And how did you manage that?"

"You should ask him yourself when you have a moment." Markham smiled as he imagined the complaints the young man would voice about how often they'd had to stop. Although to give the man his due, he hadn't protested once during their journey. That spoke volumes about his character.

"We've met before."

He gave his head a shake. She must be mistaken. "That isn't possible. He's been on the continent, engaged in the war, for several years. Unless you knew him before he enlisted?"

She removed her glasses as she considered her response. His alarm grew with each passing second.

"I met him in London the night before you told me I had to return home."

Somehow Markham kept his composure, although

it was a near thing. "Would you care to explain the details? Tell me he didn't see you in that tavern."

When Amelia refused to meet his gaze, Markham wanted nothing more than to swear.

"I looked different than I do know. I don't think he recognized me."

Which explained why Amelia had her hair covered and was wearing her reading glasses. He'd only seen her don the latter when it was late, and never unless she was reading or writing.

"He intervened when one of the other patrons tried to take liberties. We escaped out the back door, and he arranged for the carriage to take me home while he returned to his friends."

This time he did swear. He never did so in front of his clients, but Amelia had long since become more than that. She was family, which meant she saw the real man hidden behind his persona of elderly family solicitor.

"I told you pretending to be a barmaid was dangerous. Why did he even need to *intervene*, as you say? I made arrangements to ensure you were safe."

"You did, and Alice was wonderful. She deserved the payment you gave her."

She didn't know he'd also stationed one man inside the tavern to watch over her and another outside. "And yet you still had to be saved by someone else. By the new marquess, of all people." He didn't raise his voice, but he didn't have to. Amelia knew he was displeased.

"She jumped in moments after he did. And if he hadn't been there, she would have been able to sway attention away from me."

"Do I even want to know what happened?"

She winced. "Promise you'll wait until I finish."

He wanted to protest but knew she'd withhold the details from him. He waved his hand to indicate she should proceed.

"It was difficult, of course, serving customers. I wasn't as fast as the other barmaids, but Alice was a godsend. She helped me a great deal. Even lied to the owner of the tavern about who I was. One of the other barmaids wanted an evening off. Alice told the owner the woman was home, ill, and that I was her cousin who'd agreed to take her place. The man didn't care as long as I did my job."

"Which you did, of course." Amelia had always been quick at learning new skills. Although he hated the idea that barmaid in a tavern was now one of those skills.

Amelia gave her head a little shake. "I was terrible at first. But I did improve as the evening progressed."

"And Lowenbrock?"

"He arrived with two friends. They were a lively group, but they were respectful toward Alice. They were more intent on talking than bothering the barmaids."

Another point in the marquess's favor. You could tell a lot about a man's character by how he treated those who were beneath his station.

"I didn't serve them, and I don't think he even noticed me. I was responsible for the tables in the other half of the room. At any rate, it was nearing midnight when a group of men I'd been serving became rowdy. A few propositioned me, but I was able to hold them off with a few teasing words as Alice had taught me."

He never should have assisted her in setting up this insane scheme, but he'd had little choice in the matter. Amelia was stubborn enough to proceed on her own, and so he'd convinced himself that helping was the only way to ensure no harm came to her. He opened his mouth to say something about how he should have tried harder to stop her, but she held up a finger.

"You promised to allow me to finish. Or at least you implied that you agreed."

She was right and so he waited, unable to keep the frown from his face.

"It was fine, Mr. Markham. Nothing I couldn't handle. Or so I thought until someone pulled me onto their lap."

"What!" For a moment, he feared his ancient heart would stop. When it kicked before starting to thud loudly, he had visions of collapsing and leaving this young woman alone in the world. This woman who was so smart when it came to learning but so naive when it came to the motivations of men.

"It was over almost as soon as it started. Lord Lowenbrock was suddenly there, and he pulled me away from the man and placed himself between us. For a moment I thought they were going to come to blows, but then Alice swooped in and told me I was needed in the kitchens. She did an admirable job of distracting the man who'd... Well, you know."

Markham closed his eyes for several moments, the entire scene playing out in his mind. Some lout had tried to have his way with her. If he frequented the tavern regularly, Alice would know who he was. And if that was the case, Markham would exact his revenge. His clients were composed solely of those among the upper class, but he also possessed a vast network of associates who had access to all manner of information. That information included who to contact if one needed to teach someone a lesson.

Yes, a beating should do nicely. With a warning never to force his attentions on women who didn't want it.

When he looked at her again, she seemed of two minds about continuing. He schooled his features and said, "Please continue."

She glanced toward the drawing room door and continued in a volume barely loud enough for him to hear. "He escorted me out the back exit and then arranged for his carriage to take me to your town house. Alone. He returned to his friends. He thought I was someone called Molly. Between the hair covering and my glasses, and the fact it was dark in the tavern and again outside, I'm hoping he won't realize Molly and I are the same person."

He wanted to chastise her for putting herself in danger, but he needed to proceed with caution. Amelia had developed an independent streak in the years since her uncle's death, and if he wasn't careful, she would proceed on her next adventure without telling anyone. His thoughts shied away from images of everything that could happen—and often did—to a young woman on her own.

"Please tell me you don't plan on repeating that night's ill-conceived actions."

Amelia's lips pressed together before she let out a soft sigh. "I'm afraid that night's events shook me a great deal. In future, I'll limit my research to interviewing others instead of stepping into their roles directly."

He could feel his tense muscles begin to relax. Interviews wouldn't be so bad. She'd probably learn things a properly raised woman shouldn't, but it was better than experiencing them for herself.

"You'll probably need to remain here for some time. Maybe later in the year you can come down and visit. I must admit, I've grown accustomed to having you around."

Amelia shook her head. "I was always underfoot,

asking a million questions, and you were relieved to return to the quiet of your home. Admit it."

How was this young woman so astute? "Never."

She laughed. "I'll miss you too. Do you know when you'll be leaving?"

"I thought I'd stay a day or two. These old bones can't handle too much travel these days, and the trip from London is a long one." He closed one eye in a teasing wink, and she laughed.

He hated to admit, even to himself, that there was more than an ounce of truth to the statement. Gone were the days of traveling all over England to visit his clients. Fortunately, he'd been able to transition most of his clients to the younger members of his firm. Lowenbrock was his last remaining client, and he planned to continue overseeing matters pertaining to the marquisate as long as Amelia wasn't settled.

His thoughts returned to the young man who'd taken over the estate. At seven and twenty, he was only two years older than Amelia. He was pleasing enough to look at, and it appeared his character was above reproach. Perhaps the formerly impoverished John Evans could step in and take over that role for him, and not just as Amelia's guardian.

There was definitely something in the air between the marquess and Amelia. But given what she'd told him about the events at the tavern, it would be best if they proceeded slowly.

Yes, he'd have to keep an eye on these two. He

imagined that his young charge was intent on avoiding the marquess. He'd have to bring them together to see whether there was a spark of attraction between them.

He stood when Amelia excused herself and settled back into his chair. Yes, perhaps he'd finally see Amelia settled and the new marquess on the way to producing the heir that was so desperately needed.

CHAPTER 9

*A*MELIA SCOWLED AT THE LACE CAP and spectacles that rested on top of her dressing table. She'd discarded them as soon as she returned to her bedroom, but she could no longer ignore them. It was time to go downstairs for dinner.

A large part of her wanted to avoid Lowenbrock, and she considered excusing herself with a headache and asking for a tray to be sent up to her room. But the logical side of her nature wouldn't allow her to hide. Once he became accustomed to her presence, he'd discard any notion she could be the barmaid Molly.

As she reached for the cap and spectacles she hoped would conceal their prior acquaintance, she told herself she wouldn't have to wear them forever. It was too soon for her to appear as she normally did. After some time had passed, his memory of that night would fade. If he did think about the barmaid he'd met and wondered about her resemblance to Molly, he'd assume he wasn't remembering the details of that evening clearly. He'd been drinking after all.

But for tonight it was too soon to tempt fate. With a sigh, she pinned the white cap in place and perched the reading glasses on her nose. Her maid had already helped her dress for dinner in a pale blue dress that flowed loose about her figure.

Pushing down the nerves that fluttered in her belly, Amelia made her way to the drawing room. When she arrived, both Lowenbrock and Mr. Markham were waiting for her. They stood when she entered the room, and she took in the marquess's formal attire. His dark blue coat and waistcoat served to accentuate the man's good looks. His blond hair, while short, had a hint of curl that gave him a boyish quality that only added to his appeal.

She dipped into a curtsy. "I hope I haven't kept you waiting."

"Not at all," Mr. Markham said. "I've only just come down myself."

Lowenbrock smiled his welcome, one corner of his mouth hiking up higher than the other. Amelia was grateful she'd never been one to blush or lose her composure when faced with an attractive man. The marquess was probably accustomed to rendering women into tittering fools, but she was determined not to be one of those women.

Still, she found herself at a loss as to what to say. The moment of awkwardness passed quickly though when a footman arrived to announce the meal was ready to be served.

"It appears your timing is excellent," Lowenbrock said.

"One of the advantages of being raised in this house. I'm well acquainted with how it's run."

Lowenbrock held out his arm, and she hesitated a moment before taking it. She chastised herself for being silly. She'd done this many times with her uncle, and even, on occasion, with other young men, although never with someone to whom she felt an attraction. The situation left her more than a little unsettled.

She tried not to think about the romantic notions she'd developed for this man after he'd saved her and escorted her to his carriage so she could be delivered home safely. Her thoughts that night had been filled with what-ifs. But even as she spun fairy-tale scenarios in her mind, she hadn't allowed her fantasies to carry her away. Instead, she'd used those fantasies as inspiration for the characters in the book she was currently writing. Now she found herself in the uncomfortable position of having to remind herself that the character she'd created wasn't this man at all. And Amelia certainly wasn't her heroine.

She found it difficult to remind herself of that fact as she gazed up at him where he stood next to her, looking impossibly handsome as he smiled down at her before leading her from the room.

When he leaned down to whisper something in her ear, she held her breath.

"You'll have to help me find the dining room. I'm not used to living in such a large house, and I'm afraid I haven't learned the layout yet."

Amelia released her breath with a small huff of laughter as she discreetly tugged his arm to indicate they should turn right at the central foyer.

Dinner was more elaborate than normal. It was clear that Cook was trying to impress the new marquess. She made a mental note to ask Lowenbrock about his preferences so she could adjust the menus while he was in residence. She didn't normally eat such a large meal in the evening, but she knew that men tended to have heartier appetites. Especially when they were so broad and muscular...

She gave her head a slight shake to clear it of wayward thoughts. Later, when she was making notes for her book, she could allow herself all manner of fancy. But right now she had to keep from embarrassing herself.

"How are you finding the estate?" Mr. Markham asked.

Lowenbrock furrowed his brow. "Massive. I lost my way when coming down for dinner. One of the maids found me wandering in the east wing. Or at least I think it was the east wing. It might have been the west wing. North? South?"

Amelia couldn't hold back a giggle, delighted the man had a sense of humor.

"It wasn't amusing at all, I assure you. I thought I was going to perish, never to be seen or heard from again."

Mr. Markham lifted one brow but kept his expression serious. "After all the effort it took to find the next Marquess of Lowenbrock, you can rest assured I would have found you when you didn't appear for dinner."

"It's true," Amelia said. "At one point Mr. Markham despaired of finding an heir. I still remember the letter he sent when he found you. Although that letter was lacking in detail. I imagined you'd be much older and portly."

This time it was Lowenbrock's turn to laugh. "That might describe me in a few years if I keep eating like this. I'm going to have to be careful now that I'm no longer in the army."

The rest of the meal passed with companionable chatter. When the last plate was taken away, they all stood. Amelia was about to leave the gentlemen to their after-dinner chatter, but Mr. Markham put an end to that notion.

"It's been a long day for me. I think I'll retire to my room and give the two of you some time to become acquainted."

He nodded to Lowenbrock and then turned to Amelia and took her hand, placing a kiss in the air above her wrist. Amelia wondered at his sudden formality, but when his eyes met hers, the mischievous twinkle in them told her he'd anticipated her desire to escape. The marquess's gaze was on them, however, so she couldn't ask Mr. Markham what he hoped to gain from this pretense. He should be helping her to avoid Lowenbrock, not pushing them to spend more time together.

When Mr. Markham left the room, she turned back to the marquess. "You've had a long day as well. You don't have to entertain me if you'd rather retire."

John's eyes crinkled with amusement. "Given the long days I had while in the army, today was hardly taxing."

It appeared she wouldn't be escaping this man just yet. She only hoped her luck would hold and he wouldn't recognize her from their first meeting.

"Let us retire to the drawing room then."

He fell into step beside her.

"I'm glad we have this opportunity to talk," he said as they made their way down the hallway. "There's something I wanted to ask you."

Dread settled in the pit of her stomach. *Please don't ask me if I've recently been to London,* she thought. It was one thing keeping the truth from him, but something entirely different lying to him. She tried to be truthful whenever possible, and if he asked her that question, she would have no choice but to confess.

When he settled into one of the drawing room chairs, she took a seat on the settee. She folded her hands on her lap and tried to appear calm. Inside, however, her emotions were in turmoil.

"I spent the time after I left you this afternoon going through a seemingly endless amount of paper. Records, lists of properties, accounts. None of it in depth, of course. That will take considerably more time."

Relief coursed through her when she realized the secret of their first meeting would remain safe for yet another day.

"Uncle always said that going over the accounts with Mr. Jeffers was an endless task."

John let out a breath. "Yes, and that's another thing. I know the man is away on business and I haven't met him yet. But I'll admit I'm already feeling overwhelmed. I'd like to ask for your assistance."

Amelia nodded. "Of course. I'd be more than happy to continue in my role running the household. I plan to revise the menus according to your likes and dislikes. And if there's anything else you need, you have only to ask."

"Markham told me earlier that you did more than oversee the menus and household staff. When your uncle fell ill, Markham took you under his wing and showed you how to run the estate. I'd like to ask that you do the same for me."

Her thoughts blanked for a moment. What he was suggesting meant they'd spend a great deal of time together.

"If it's not too much to ask, of course. Markham spoke highly about your skills. If there are any tasks you enjoy doing, I have no issue with your continuing to do them. But if you hate all of it, I only ask that you have a little patience with me before dumping all the duties into my lap and escaping. I can't say I would blame you."

"I—" Amelia had no idea what to say. And so she told him that exactly.

One corner of Lowenbrock's mouth lifted. "Let's begin with this. Can I come to you if I have any questions?"

"Of course, but you've taken me by surprise. There aren't many men who would welcome guidance from a woman."

"Well, my eldest sister is seven years older than me. A fair portion of my life was spent listening to her tell me what to do."

His statement had her wondering about his family's composition. "And your mother?"

"My mother died when I was still a babe. I don't remember her. But my sister Louisa more than made up for her absence."

Amelia's heart wrenched. "I'm sorry to hear that.

My parents both died when I was still a youth. That's why I came here to live with my uncle."

John's gaze softened in sympathy. "My father was ill just before I went into the army. His death was one of the things that precipitated my decision to enlist."

There was something in the way he looked away as he said that last bit that had Amelia wondering about the other reasons. She wasn't about to pry, however. If he didn't tell her, it was because he didn't want her to know.

She pushed her glasses up from where they had slid on her nose. "I'd be more than happy to offer my assistance wherever possible."

"Good," he said. "We can start tomorrow morning."

"So soon? Why the rush?"

"Markham tells me Jeffers will be returning tomorrow afternoon. While I'm versed in mathematics, I never learned how to keep accounts. I thought you could help me make sense of them so I won't embarrass myself when I meet him."

"Mr. Jeffers would be happy to go over them in detail with you."

Lowenbrock hesitated and Amelia waited, wondering what he was thinking.

Finally he released his breath. "It's silly, I know, but I don't want to appear lacking. It might be because of my years in the army, where to show weakness meant you were the subject of endless ridicule.

Or perhaps the fact that I grew up in *genteel poverty*." His mouth turned down for a moment. "It's probably a combination of both, but I'd rather not appear as though I don't belong here even if that's the case."

His honesty humbled her. "You belong here, my lord. Of that I have no doubt."

Lowenbrock's gaze settled on hers for several long moments. "I'd like to be friends, Miss Weston."

She felt a twinge of guilt about her deceit. "Of course."

"Then maybe we can dispense with the 'my lords.'"

For a moment she was shocked by his request, but when she considered his upbringing, she found she couldn't blame him. He'd lived his life never expecting to become a member of the nobility, let alone a marquess. He was only one step below a duke.

She chewed on her lip and stopped immediately when she saw the way his eyes zeroed in on her mouth. Her uncle had hated that habit. She'd taught herself to stop doing it, but in the years since his passing had fallen into the practice again.

"Should I call you Lowenbrock?"

"If you must. I might not answer you right away though. I'm still not used to the title. It will probably feel as though you're referring to someone else."

She opened her mouth to say something about understanding how that felt but then snapped it closed again. Horror settled over her when she realized she'd almost admitted how difficult it had been for her to answer to the name Molly.

She pulled her scattered thoughts together before saying, "It will be strange for me, as well. Lowenbrock was my uncle."

"Perhaps, in time, you can use my given name. It's what I'm used to, after all. I've never been anything but John to my family and Evans to my fellow officers."

She felt a little thrill go through her at his request. She'd never be able to call him by his Christian name, however. That felt too intimate. "We'll try Lowenbrock for now. You'll be accustomed to it before you know it."

"I don't have any choice in the matter." He gave his head a small shake as though to clear the strange mood that had settled over him. "At any rate, perhaps we can start after breakfast tomorrow? Markham can join us as well. The two of you can fill in the gaps in my knowledge so I don't come out looking like a fool before my steward."

"We'll see you then. Breakfast is normally served at eight, but I know that is early. I can ask the staff to serve later in the morning."

"Eight works for me. I'm normally up a little earlier, but that will give me the opportunity to visit the stables. Perhaps I'll be able to choose a horse and go for a ride." One corner of his mouth lifted, and his eyes lit with amusement as he continued. "I do need to get a start on working off these excellent meals after all. I don't want to become that portly gentleman you imagined."

Amelia smiled in response to his jest. "The staff is efficient and loyal. You needn't concern yourself that it will be difficult to settle in."

"I've never been head of a household before. You'll have to ensure I stay on the correct path. Let me know if I'm being too soft on them. Or heaven forbid, too much of a tyrant."

She shook her head. "I doubt the latter is possible."

He inclined his head. "I'll see you tomorrow morning then, at eight."

She stood, and he did as well. "I look forward to it."

As she swept from the room, she realized that statement was truer than she'd imagined possible when she first learned the new Marquess of Lowenbrock would soon be in residence. It was easy being in the man's presence. He had a way of putting one at ease without too much effort. She would have to be careful. She'd already come close to betraying herself with no prodding on his part.

CHAPTER 10

THE STABLE MASTER WASN'T EXAGGERATING when he told John the light bay gelding was more than up to the task of a brisk ride. They'd already gone a fair distance that morning, and the animal showed no signs of tiring. But he didn't want to be late for breakfast, so all too soon he brought the horse around and headed back.

As he came closer to his new home, he was surprised to realize he felt no regret about returning to Brock Manor and his new life as lord. He wasn't sure to what he could attribute that fact. In London he'd put off meeting with Markham as long as possible because he'd dreaded having to acknowledge his life was about to change so completely.

He would always remember the day he'd received that letter from Louisa disclosing the news that the Lowenbrock title and all its holdings were now his. If it had come from anyone else—even Catherine—he wouldn't have believed it. He would have thought they were having one over on him. For a moment, he'd wondered if he was dreaming. But while he knew his older sister wanted nothing more than for him to give up his commission and return to England, she wouldn't lie about something like that.

That was three years ago. Louisa had implored him to return to London on several occasions, pleas he'd chosen to ignore. But once Napoleon had been defeated, he'd seen far too much of war and longed to return to the English countryside. When his closest friends disclosed their own plans to return home, he'd joined them and resigned his commission.

For the first time since returning to England, he felt like he was finally home. Being in the country again, away from the bustle of London, reminded him of his youth. His family had lived in a cottage instead of the large manse he now owned, but there was something about the clean air and quiet solitude of country life that he'd missed with a bone-deep ache. The fact that he was in Yorkshire instead of Kent mattered now. He was finally home. He couldn't remember the last time he'd felt so comfortable in his own skin.

The dichotomy between his joy at returning to the English countryside and his unease with the reality that he was now a member of the ton pulled him in opposite directions. But for right now, in that very moment, he knew he could be happy here.

He guided his mount to the stables, dismounted, and allowed one of the grooms to lead the horse away. Normally he would have taken the time to see to the animal's care himself, but he was already running late. He wouldn't have time to wash the smell of horse from himself before breakfast.

He hoped Miss Weston wouldn't take offense. She was going out of her way to help him after all.

He strode toward the house and was unnerved when the front door opened just as he reached it. But there was no magic involved. A veritable army of servants were now at his beck and call. He tried not to let that thought unsettle him. They were ordinary people like him, doing their best to get on with their lives.

John's thoughts turned to Miss Weston as he thanked the butler and handed the man his hat and gloves. It bothered him how much she reminded him of the barmaid he'd helped. *Rescued,* his friends had teased.

Of course, he could only remember general details about the woman. She'd had dark brown hair that curled slightly, blue eyes, and a generous mouth. While he didn't know if Miss Weston's hair curled or fell straight, she shared the other features. She was also of similar height, but most women were slight when compared to his own six feet. Half the women in England possessed those same features.

The events of that evening had passed so quickly he couldn't even be certain he was remembering the barmaid correctly. It was possible that what he'd observed of the young woman with whom he was sharing the estate was coloring his memories of Molly.

He brought his mind back to the present when Hastings informed him that Miss Weston had already come down and then gave him directions to the breakfast room. Apparently it was adjacent to the dining room where they'd eaten the night before.

With a word of thanks, he made his way down the hall. He wouldn't examine why his spirits lightened with each step he took.

Amelia was seated and halfway through her breakfast when he entered the room. "Good morning, my lord." When he raised a brow in response, she sighed. "Good morning, Lowenbrock."

"This is quite the feast," he said as he moved to the sideboard to make a plate for himself. He took no shame in piling it high, wanting to sample each item that was served. He returned to the table and took a seat next to her. "Surely we don't need quite so much for the two of us and Markham. Has he already come down?"

Amelia shook her head. "He asked for something to be sent to his room. He sent his excuses, saying he's still feeling fatigued after your long journey."

She took her lower lip between her teeth, and John had to force himself to look away when he realized he was wondering what those lips would taste like.

"I may have been too hard on him. I'll admit to wondering at times if he was trying to delay me."

Amelia coughed at that. "I think he's starting to feel his age. He used to visit several times a year, but it's been a long time since he's visited Brock Manor. I worry about him."

"I wondered why he's still practicing law."

"I think that's for me. My uncle had him promise to look after me, and he's taken to the role of honorary uncle with ease. Perhaps once you've settled in here, he'll feel comfortable recommending another solicitor to take over the estate's legal matters."

He didn't miss the way her lips turned down slightly at the thought. "You'll miss his visits."

"He's been very kind to me. Whatever I needed, he was there to help me. And he never made me feel as though I was a duty he had to bear."

"Even if he steps down from being my solicitor, there's no reason we won't be able to see him from time to time."

She gave him an odd look that he couldn't decipher. When she said nothing further, he dug into his breakfast, starting first with the plum cake.

A full minute of companionable silence passed before Amelia pushed her plate away. "Cook cannot continue to prepare this much food. I know the staff will have a feast with the leftovers, but it is wasteful. I'll speak to her about moderating her output."

"I have no issue with the servants enjoying a good breakfast. They shouldn't have to wait for us to eat first though."

Amelia smiled. "Try telling that to Mrs. Hastings. She runs this household on a tight schedule and insists the staff will get lazy if we coddle them too much."

John frowned. "Should I be concerned about how she treats them? I won't have it said that I run my staff into the ground."

"Oh no, you needn't concern yourself on that account. Make no mistake, they're not deprived and eat well. It's just that there isn't normally quite so much left over for the servants to enjoy. We could all eat for a week on what Cook has served this morning!"

"I'm glad to hear that."

She watched him closely for several seconds before speaking. "You've no doubt guessed that the butler and head housekeeper are married. Do you have any concerns about that?"

She was chewing on that damn lower lip again, and he had to resist the urge to tell her to stop.

"As long as their relationship doesn't interfere with

their management of the household, I don't see that my opinion matters one way or the other."

"I'm so glad to hear that. They wed with Uncle's blessing just before he passed away. Mrs. Hastings mentioned at that time that other households would discourage the relationship."

John gave his head a confused shake. "To what end? Their relationship would continue; they'd just do a better job of hiding it. And secrets are never a good thing. Better to have everything out in the open."

CHAPTER 11

*S*HE FROZE AT LOWENBROCK'S WORDS and had to remind herself to continue breathing. His words felt as though they'd been aimed directly at her.

For a moment she considered telling him the truth about their first meeting but quickly discarded the notion. Markham's haste to have her return to Yorkshire and his warning that the future marquess mustn't learn about her research trip to London kept playing in her mind. Lowenbrock might not approve of her continuing to live at Brock Manor if he thought she made a habit of frequenting taverns.

She looked down at her plate and picked up the toast she'd abandoned, nibbling on it as an excuse to remain silent.

She'd only been inside a tavern that one time and for very good reason, but he might not believe her.

She'd told him that Markham had promised to look after her. It would follow, therefore, that Lowenbrock might think he was lying on her behalf if questioned about that evening.

This entire situation was a mess. She peeked up at Lowenbrock and watched as he brought a forkful of eggs to his mouth with relish. He seemed like a reasonable person. Perhaps he would understand. "Some people might have good reasons for keeping a secret."

He frowned at her but said nothing.

She took another bite of her toast. It appeared she would get no indication from him as to whether it was safe to tell him about their first meeting. Perhaps after some time had passed, once he got to know her better, he wouldn't think ill of her after learning the truth.

It was time to change the subject. "When did you want to start going over the accounts?"

The way he looked at her—as though she were his saving grace—had a strange effect on her. She would have been a fool not to notice how handsome this man was. It was the reason, after all, that she'd modeled the hero in her book after him. But her appreciation went far beyond the acknowledgment of his external appearance. She was drawn to him in a way that was far from wise.

"I'll need to wash up first. I apologize for coming straight from the stables, but I didn't want to keep you waiting."

She waved a hand in dismissal. "Such is country life. You needn't apologize to me. I have a few things I need to do before we meet."

She ignored the way her stomach dipped at his smile of thanks and stood. He followed suit, and she couldn't help but notice, again, just how tall he was.

She glanced down at his plate, which still contained a large quantity of food. "I hope you enjoy the rest of your breakfast. You can send a footman to let me know when you're ready."

He gave her a formal bow. She dipped into a curtsy and exited the room, letting out a large sigh when she reached the hallway.

She'd wanted to tell him that he didn't need to apologize because he smelled wonderful. Yes, he did smell like horses, but the combination of his own scent and that of the outdoors left her feeling slightly light-headed.

No, it was best she keep that information to herself. She couldn't guarantee that detail wouldn't make its way into her book, however.

CHAPTER 12

JOHN'S MEETING WITH THE ESTATE STEWARD was decidedly less enjoyable than the morning he'd spent with Miss Weston. Yes, he and Amelia had spent that time going over the same material in detail, but the company had been more agreeable to him.

Mr. Raymond Jeffers was a middle-aged man who droned on a little too long, sharing details about day-to-day matters that John wouldn't be able to remember. And Jeffers spoke in a monotone that had the effect of lulling him into thoughts of going back to bed.

At least he could ask Amelia to go over the many subjects the steward seemed intent on covering in this one meeting.

John cut him off when he threatened to go into excessive detail about the crops. "You mentioned that repairs to some of the cottages are needed. Why haven't they been completed yet?"

Jeffers looked at him as though he'd lost his mind. "There was no marquess over the past few years."

John ignored the twinge of guilt that hit him at those words. It wasn't an accusation, but it felt like one. "Your point being?"

Jeffers removed his spectacles and pinched the bridge of his nose before replacing them. "I wanted to make the repairs, and Miss Weston encouraged me to proceed. Your solicitor, however, cautioned me against any expenses that might be seen by some as being excessive."

John frowned at what he considered the unnecessary delay. "What exactly did Markham think you had in mind?"

"Nothing beyond patching roofs and walls. The standard repairs that need to be seen to over time. One or two of the cottages might need to be replaced altogether."

"And you allowed the tenants to live under those conditions?" John winced inwardly when he realized he'd spoken more sharply than he'd intended. But given that his family had lived in near poverty before his sister had wed the Marquess of Overlea and he'd enlisted, he couldn't help but feel outraged at the thought of his tenants suffering from neglect.

"We didn't know who would inherit. It's no secret that many members of society don't care about the living conditions of their tenants as long as their own income isn't affected. We had no way of knowing whether the next marquess would feel the same way."

"Well, I don't. Please see to it that the repairs are conducted right away. And that includes building new cottages where necessary."

Jeffers narrowed his eyes, his expression impassive. "That might cost more than you imagine."

John waved a hand over the account books. "I'm sure it won't bankrupt me, and I won't have my tenants neglected."

"I'll see to it right away, my lord."

Jeffers did something completely unexpected then. He smiled. It was the first genuine emotion the man had exhibited, and John couldn't help but feel that he'd passed some sort of test.

CHAPTER 13

*A*MELIA KNEW SHE WAS RISKING DISCOVERY by continuing to do her writing in the library. It was her favorite room in the house, however, and she could spread out the pages of her manuscript on the desk she'd set up in one corner of the room, next to a large window that looked out on the back gardens. Mrs. Brambles lay on a cushion next to the window, her customary location whenever Amelia was writing.

Conscious of the need to tread with care, she limited herself to a small, neat stack of pages. The notes she'd made about the next few scenes in the book were facedown beside her, but she didn't need to glance at them that afternoon. The words flowed from her fingers in an unending stream, the scene fully formed in her head.

The sound of the door being opened had her raising her head to find Lowenbrock had entered the room. Fortunately, she'd prepared for this eventuality. She'd written a page of instructions for Mrs. Hastings about household matters they needed to discuss.

She smiled her welcome as she took that list and placed it on top of the pages of her manuscript. Lowenbrock would think she was making notes on household matters if he glanced at it.

He hovered just inside the doorway. "I didn't mean to interrupt. I can come back later if you're busy."

"Not at all. I was just finishing."

"Do you mind if I join you then? I promise to be quiet as you work."

His expression was so earnest, and it elicited a strange need in her to comfort him. No doubt he was feeling overwhelmed after his meeting with Jeffers. The man did have the effect of wearing one out with his insistence on covering every detail.

"Of course not," she said, setting the pages aside.

As though to add her agreement, Mrs. Brambles stretched and made her way over to Lowenbrock, where she rubbed against the man's legs before quitting the room. No doubt in search of another quiet place where her nap wouldn't be interrupted.

"I think she likes you more than she does me."

One corner of Lowenbrock's mouth lifted as he settled into a comfortable chair. "If that was the case, she wouldn't be sleeping next to you."

Amelia rose from her chair at the desk and moved

to join him. When he started to stand, she lifted a hand to stop him. He stood anyway.

"That will grow tiresome if you insist on standing whenever I do."

"Perhaps I won't feel the need after some time has passed. But for now…" He shrugged.

And of course this man, who thought nothing of rescuing barmaids he didn't know, would never disrespect a gently bred woman. She settled into a chair opposite him, and he relaxed back into his seat.

"It has only been a few hours since I left your study, and you appear exhausted."

His eyes narrowed on her in accusation. "You could have warned me about Jeffers. The man spent a full thirty minutes talking about the weather and its effect on the various crops. The weather! It is England in the springtime. It is either cloudy or it's raining."

Amelia couldn't hold back her laughter at his mock outrage. "Well, it has been an abnormally cool spring. And the man is passionate about his responsibilities. I'm sure he just wanted you to know the estate is in capable hands. But he's sweet, as is his wife."

Lowenbrock leaned back in his chair. "If you say so. I did manage to get one smile out of him."

"High praise indeed! Mr. Jeffers doesn't give his approval easily. Make no mistake, he would continue to do his job even if you were a tyrant, but I'm glad to hear the two of you are getting along."

"Yes, well, there is another matter I wanted to speak to you about."

Amelia forced herself not to glance back to the desk where several pages of her manuscript rested. Instead, she pushed her spectacles farther up her nose and attempted to look as though his words didn't set off a spark of alarm within her. "I am at your service."

He frowned at her choice of words. "You don't need to be. This is your home as well as mine for as long as you want it to be. I don't want you to feel as though you have to earn your position here."

This man was going to be the death of her. After their first interaction, she had already built him up as a paragon in her mind, and now he was doing everything in his power to make her feel secure.

If she wasn't careful, she'd be in danger of losing her heart to him. Somehow she needed to channel these feelings into her heroine without falling victim to them herself. Especially since the new marquess showed no signs of seeing her as anything but a duty he needed to fulfill.

"I appreciate your assurances. But this is no ordeal for me. I'm used to seeing to whatever needs to be done, and I have never resented that fact. You needn't feel as though you are imposing."

His gaze fixed on her. "Would you tell me if I was?"

"I'd like to think so."

He relaxed again, and she could tell she'd set his mind at ease.

Markham wandered into the library with a slight harrumph. "So this is where the two of you have been hiding."

"We're hardly hiding," Amelia said in reply. She saw the way his gaze took in the papers on the desk before he looked away. From the significant look he gave her, he knew she'd been writing.

He pulled out the desk chair and brought it to their sitting area. "What are we talking about?"

John let out an exaggerated breath. "I've received a large number of calling cards, and I'm not sure what to do about them. I don't have time to visit with every resident of Yorkshire."

She raised a shoulder in a casual shrug. "Are you surprised? Everyone is curious about the new marquess and wants to make your acquaintance."

Markham shook his head, his expression indulgent. "Is that what you believe? That they're curious about the new Lord Lowenbrock?"

Amelia tilted her head to one side as she tried to discern the meaning behind the solicitor's words. "What else could it be? I know I was filled with curiosity—which you wouldn't indulge."

Lowenbrock frowned. "Are they planning to gawk at me and judge whether I'll live up to the title?"

"Oh, I have no doubt that's part of it. But I'm

sure most of those cards are from men who have a more personal reason for calling."

Amelia wished he would just say what he was thinking. "And what reason would that be?"

"No doubt many, if not most of them, have unattached daughters who are of age or nearing it. Some will want to see if Lord Lowenbrock would be an appropriate match for those daughters. Others won't care, they'll just want to ensure their family is aligned with his."

Mr. Markham's words made sense, and she couldn't stop the dread that hollowed out her stomach at the thought. "So soon? He just took up residence yesterday."

"The early bird gets the worm. I'm sure all the matchmaking mamas within a reasonable distance have urged their male family members to make your acquaintance as soon as possible, my lord."

Lowenbrock was silent for several moments. From the way his jaw tightened, Amelia could tell he wanted to say something. Curiosity overcame her when he remained silent.

"What are you thinking?"

"I'm trying to keep from swearing aloud. My thoughts right now are not fit for delicate sensibilities."

Amelia resisted the urge to tell him not to hold back on her account. She'd heard all manner of rude speech that one night in London.

He leaned back in his chair and closed his eyes. "I thought I'd escaped that nonsense when I quit London. My sisters were starting to make plans to parade me around the marriage mart. Apparently it followed me here."

"You are a titled gentleman with great wealth," Mr. Markham said. "There is nowhere for you to hide save in marriage."

He glanced at Amelia, and it suddenly occurred to her what he was doing. The man was matchmaking. She gave him a reproving glare. Instead of being chastened, however, he smiled at her, unrepentant.

Amelia wet her lips before asking, "What are your plans with respect to marriage?"

Lowenbrock leaned forward to rest his elbows on his knees, locking his gaze on her. "*Et tu, Brute?* Have you already picked out my bride from amongst the neighboring families?"

She couldn't hold back her snort and didn't miss the way his eyes widened at her reaction. "I'm sorry, my lord, but you forget that I've met those families. I wouldn't do that to you. You'll have to look farther afield to find a bride, I'm afraid."

"Or much closer to home."

Markham's words were softly spoken and meant for her. Her gaze flew to him then back to the marquess.

"What was that?" Lowenbrock asked.

Amelia released her breath. He hadn't heard, thank goodness.

"Nothing of import," Mr. Markham said. "I was just thinking about something I needed to do. I'll go and handle that now." He rose and started for the door. He took only two steps before he stopped and turned to face them again. "You should host a ball. That will give everyone the chance to meet you and take your measure. It will be tedious, I'm sure, since every unwed female present will have their sights set on you. But it's best to get it over with all at once."

He strode from the room with a jaunty step that belied his advanced age.

This time Lowenbrock didn't hold back his soft curse.

Amelia looked at him with sympathy. "I'm afraid he might be correct. If what you said is true and you're already receiving calls, then they won't leave you alone until they've had the chance to speak with you. After which they'll be inviting you to their homes to meet their families. Best to gather them all in one place and meet everyone at once."

"Do we even have a ballroom?"

The look of disbelief she cast his way was her only reply.

"Of course we do. The house is certainly large enough." Lowenbrock shook his head. "I won't be able to stand there while all the guests stare at me. I'll never survive having that much attention centered on me." Lowenbrock's eyes narrowed on her. "You're looking forward to this."

Amelia laughed. "I must admit that I am. We may be far from town, but that doesn't mean we don't enjoy our balls. And it will be amusing to watch everyone tie themselves in knots to ensnare your favor."

"I feel as though I should be preparing for the hangman's noose."

She laughed at his expression of exaggerated dismay. "Oh, don't be so melodramatic."

"Fine, we'll have a ball. But if we're doing this, we'll do it up right. That means I'll be inviting my two sisters and their families. And while we're at it, I have a couple of friends I'd like to invite. They're of an age with me and also titled and unwed. They can share in the unwanted attention."

Amelia wondered if he was referring to the men she'd seen him with at the tavern. She couldn't ask, however. She'd just have to wait and see.

She rose, amused at the alacrity with which he followed suit.

"Are you running off to start planning?"

"Actually," she said, moving over to her desk and gathering up her papers, "I was going to meet with the housekeeper about other household matters. I'll make sure to mention that we'll be holding a ball at some point in the near future. I can't remember the last time the ballroom was used, and she'll want to ensure every inch of the room is sparkling for the occasion."

"I can't believe I'm actually doing this." Lowenbrock stood tall, his hands clasped behind his back. "So much for trying to hold on to my sanity by leaving London before the season started."

Tamping down on her desire to lay a reassuring hand on his arm, she held the papers to her chest. A barrier to remind herself she couldn't get too close to this man. "We'll discuss dates later, after I've had a chance to talk to Mrs. Hastings."

He let out an exaggerated sigh, and she found herself laughing again as she exited the library.

CHAPTER 14

SHE FOUND MR. MARKHAM waiting for her in the hallway outside their bedrooms. With a small tilt of her head to indicate he should follow, she moved past him. He remained silent as they made their way to the small sitting room at the end of the hall. The space was seldom used, and Amelia knew they wouldn't be disturbed there.

She sighed as she looked around the room, taking in the light layer of dust on the furniture. She needed to speak to the staff about cleaning the room more often since she would now be using it for her writing. She'd had a near miss in the library. She couldn't risk Lowenbrock finding her there again while she was writing. He might start to ask questions, and she didn't want to lie to him.

The sitting room wasn't so bad. It didn't have a desk upon which she could spread out the pages of her manuscript, but she could use her lap desk. The room didn't have a view of the gardens as the library did, but there were two windows that let in plenty of light. It would have to do if she didn't want to find herself sequestered in her bedroom all day.

She placed the small sheaf of papers she carried on a side table.

Mr. Markham closed the door to the room before glancing at the pages. "Is that what I think it is?" At her nod, he continued, "You need to take greater care unless you want Lowenbrock to learn about your career as an author."

Amelia slapped a hand over her mouth when she gave an indelicate snort. "You mean my aspiration to be an author. There is no guarantee I will ever sell a book."

He shrugged. "The only way to fail for certain is to give up. But I'm sure you'll succeed. You are one of the brightest people I've met. And don't forget, I did read your first novel."

"Boring as it was." Embarrassment colored her words as she remembered the criticism leveled against her book.

Mr. Markham shrugged. "It was your first novel. You'd never written one before, so it stands to reason it would need some work."

She lowered herself onto one end of the small settee while the solicitor sat on the opposite end. "I've taken the publisher's advice. The book I'm working on now will have more excitement. And I can already see where I went wrong with the first one. I take comfort in the fact I'm already growing with respect to storytelling."

"That's my girl," he said. "And you never know what will happen. You might be able to rework your first book at some point in the future and sell it."

Amelia gave her head a little shake to clear it of wishful thoughts that might never come to pass. "Never mind any of that. What do you think you're doing, trying to play matchmaker between Lowen-brock and myself? You're no better than all those men who want to make matches for their daughters."

He raised a brow. "You're mistaken if you believe that. We have the advantage, after all. You already live here, and it's clear he likes you."

Amelia frowned. "Such a tepid word. He'd need to do more than like me before he asked for my hand."

"So you've considered it?"

"Of course not." Well, not for her. She was headed in that direction between the hero Lowen-brock had inspired and the heroine of her current book. "I think that at best, he considers me a sister." She couldn't help but frown at the thought.

"We'll change that, never you worry."

"*We?* Does that mean you're staying? And I never said I wanted to change his mind about courting me."

Mr. Markham gave her that penetrating stare she

found so unsettling at times. The one that told her he could see straight through to her very thoughts. "You'll have time to decide what you want as you prepare for the ball. And no, I must return to London. I'm not sure these old bones will be up for another long trip so soon."

Amelia pushed away her disappointment. "I need to speak to Mrs. Hastings about our plans, but I'm not sure when the marquess will want to host the ball. The season is getting underway now, so it might be best if we wait until the summer."

Mr. Markham nodded. "July will be good. Parliament is supposed to sit until July second. If Lowenbrock is still in hiding when everyone returns to the country, they might just break down the doors."

The image of a mob of beautiful young women throwing themselves at Lowenbrock's feet had her frowning. And Mr. Markham's next words left her momentarily speechless.

"I'm glad to learn the new marquess is a good man. And if you can catch his eye, I'll be able to stop worrying about you."

She aimed a quelling look his way, ignoring the way his words caused a small flutter within her belly. "I know Uncle charged you with looking out for me, but I'm no longer a girl. I'm content with my life."

He didn't contradict her, but she could see that he wanted to. She knew exactly what was on his mind—what he hoped would happen between her and

Lowenbrock. And she'd be lying to herself if she said the suggestion wasn't compelling. She'd thought about what it would be like to be with him when he'd come to her aid at the tavern. It was hard to believe that had been less than one week ago. But unless she told Lowenbrock the truth about their first meeting, she would have to remain content to craft happily-ever-afters for the characters in her books.

She retrieved the small stack of pages from the side table and stood. "I should return these to my bedroom before seeking out Mrs. Hastings."

Mr. Markham held the sitting room door open for her, and she slipped down the hallway and into the refuge of her bedroom, determined not to entertain the foolhardy notion that Lowenbrock would come to care for her as more than his charge.

CHAPTER 15

une 1816

SINCE AMELIA HAD ONLY MADE USE of a few rooms after her uncle passed away, much of the house had been closed off. That included the guest bedrooms in the west wing. With plans for the ball underway, Mrs. Hastings took her to every one of those rooms so they could catalog the furnishings and ensure the rooms would be ready to receive guests. Amelia had explained that only a few of those rooms would be used for guests of the ball. But she couldn't argue when the housekeeper suggested it would be more efficient to go through all the rooms now so they would be available for the marquess's future needs.

And so, after breakfast each morning, Amelia visited some of the closed rooms with Mrs. Hastings and a selection of maids. The contents of each room were cataloged and a plan of action created for what needed to be done with respect to cleaning and updating the linens and draperies. Lowenbrock had already approved a generous amount of money for improvements, and Amelia was determined to stay within that budget. Fortunately, only a handful of rooms needed more than an airing out and thorough dusting.

When the rooms were cleaned and updated, she had to do the entire tour over again to give the head housekeeper her stamp of approval on the readiness of the rooms.

After a morning of such activity, Amelia would escape with her lap desk to the small sitting room she'd claimed for her own and continue writing her novel.

The staff knew she spent her afternoons in the sitting room, and it wouldn't be difficult for Lowenbrock to track her down. In case that occurred, she made a point of bringing her correspondence with her. If he came upon her, it wouldn't be a lie to say she was writing a letter. She was always in the middle of writing a letter to Mary, her closest friend, these days.

But after that one time when he came across her while she was writing in the library, he never sought her out. With Mr. Markham gone and Lowenbrock busy with estate matters, loneliness began to settle over her. Which was silly, of course, because she saw the marquess every morning and at dinner each evening. It was more company than she'd had since her uncle's passing.

But there was something about sharing a household with someone with whom one *could* be interacting but wasn't that made her feel more alone than if he weren't there at all.

Her writing progressed at a steady pace. It was nearing the end of June—two months after the marquess's arrival—and she had passed the midpoint of her novel. It would need extensive edits, of course, but she was ecstatic about the progress she was making. She was so immersed in her characters' lives that scenes and snippets of dialogue assailed her at odd moments throughout the day. She'd begun to carry a small notebook with her so she could capture those moments of inspiration.

She pulled it out during dinner one evening after Lowenbrock said something particularly witty, her only thought to capture the comment for the hero in her book.

"What are you writing?"

With a guilty start, she snapped the notebook closed. When she met Lowenbrock's gaze, his eyes were alight with curiosity.

She contemplated lying but discarded the idea as soon as it entered her head. Lowenbrock would learn the truth soon enough… it might as well come from her. But she couldn't tell him everything. He hadn't realized she was the barmaid he'd met in that tavern in London despite the fact she'd long since stopped wearing her spectacles every day. She'd also considered that it might be time to stop wearing the lace cap that covered her hair.

With exaggerated care, she placed the closed notebook on the table next to her, lining up the small stub of a pencil next to it. She took a deep breath. "I have a confession to make."

Lowenbrock leaned back in his chair and crossed his arms over his chest. One brow rose in question, but he didn't speak as he waited for her to continue.

After taking another deep breath, she blurted out the truth. "I'm writing a book. A work of fiction. It's been consuming me of late, and I apologize for forgetting my manners."

His expression remained blank for several moments and then the corners of his mouth rose in a smile. As happened far too often in this man's presence, her heart leaped. "That's wonderful, Miss Weston."

His rapt attention, so different from his normal polite manner, left her flustered. "Yes, well, the publishers to whom I sent my first novel didn't think so."

"And this is your second novel?"

"Yes. I hate to admit it, but I'm afraid they were correct about my first book. I can see now where I went wrong with it, and I can feel in my bones that this one is much improved."

"Hence why you've been hiding away. I've scarce seen you since Mr. Markham departed. I thought that perhaps I had offended you in some way."

When she realized her mouth was hanging open, she closed it. "No, of course not. Between writing and preparing for the ball…" No, she wouldn't be a coward, not when Lowenbrock was being honest with her. "You've been busy as well. I know that we're scarce more than acquaintances, but I welcome your friendship."

If his smile grew any wider, she would be in danger of swooning.

"Well, good, now that we have that settled, may I…?" She glanced down at her notebook, breaking the moment that had stretched between them. She was more than a little off-balance after being the subject of his intense attention.

"By all means."

The weight of his stare settled over her for several long moments before he lifted his fork again and continued with the meal. She inhaled deeply, the air filling her lungs doing nothing to calm her sudden bout of nerves, and jotted down the witticism he'd shared. When she was done, she closed the book again and resumed her own meal.

"I'll try not to do that again. But when inspiration strikes, I find I must record it lest it be forgotten in the next moment. It's almost shocking how easily distracted I can be."

"Am I a distraction, Miss Weston?"

His amusement did strange things to his face. His gray eyes were light with merriment, but there was an intensity in his gaze that left her feeling unbalanced again.

"Everything is a distraction." She'd meant to be offhand but found the statement came off with an odd, breathy quality. She looked away and took another bite of her fish.

"Will I be allowed to read this book?"

Her thoughts scattered as she tried to think of an appropriate response. If Lowenbrock read her book, she'd no longer be able to hide the fact they'd met before his arrival at the estate. For the first time, she couldn't help but consider she might have been wrong to take Mr. Markham's advice about concealing their first meeting. The marquess was not an unreasonable man. Surely he would understand the reasons behind her actions that evening.

But two months had passed. Would he be angry she'd kept this secret from him? Or would he understand she'd been worried he would ask her to leave Brock Manor because her actions had risked her reputation and, by extension, his? Now that she'd come to know him, she didn't believe he'd behave so callously.

But she couldn't forget the look on his face when

he'd expressed his dislike for secrets. That she'd kept this information from him for so long would be a strike against her. Worse, he might think she'd been laughing at him behind his back for his failure to recognize her.

"I'll take your silence as a no."

She winced as she met his gaze. "It's a 'not at present.' I'm still writing the first draft, and there's much I'll need to fix in edits."

It was only a half-truth. She knew that one day she would have to tell him about their meeting that night in the tavern. But if, like her first novel, no one wanted to publish this book, she might not have to tell him.

What was it about this man that had her wanting to avoid the possibility he might come to think ill of her?

"I'll hold you to that. I haven't had much time of late to enjoy fiction, not with all the estate records with which I've needed to familiarize myself when I'm not out visiting tenants and overseeing the land. When you're ready, however, I would be honored to read it."

She couldn't help but think this man was nearly too perfect. She'd almost expected him to pout or to insist, but instead, he respected her need for time. And his patience only served to make him more attractive.

Which, of course, brought to mind Mr. Markham's desire that she and Lowenbrock wed. She forced her thoughts away from that possibility since the marquess clearly didn't think of her in such a manner.

She looked away, uncomfortable under his intense regard. She did not need the embarrassment of Lowenbrock realizing she found him captivating. "Distract me with another subject. Please."

He let out a soft chuckle. "As a matter of fact, there was something else I wanted to speak to you about."

She took a sip of her wine and looked at him. "As long as it isn't about me, then proceed."

He glanced down at her plate with a small frown. "I've kept you from eating with my chatter. And if you don't finish, Cook might withhold dessert."

Amelia chuckled and took another bite of her fish. She wouldn't put it past the woman to do just that.

They fell into a companionable silence as they ate, but Amelia kept stealing glances at him. Their eyes met often, but thankfully there was no awkwardness. He finished first and waited for her to complete the meal as well.

Her curiosity would no longer be put off. Taking one last sip of her wine, she waved for the footman to remove their plates and begin serving their dessert course, a delicious blancmange.

"What was it you wished to discuss with me?" She took a bite of the dessert and closed her eyes in appreciation. When she opened them again, she caught a strange look on Lowenbrock's face.

He shook his head and took his own bite before meeting her gaze again. "I've been meeting with the tenants over the past month. Trying to get to know them."

She smiled. "I'm sure they appreciated that. Many of them were quite distraught when Uncle passed away, as was I. We had no way of knowing whether an heir would even be found."

She had to look away when he brought the dessert to his mouth but was unable to understand why the simple act of watching him savor the treat made her feel uncomfortable.

"Trust me when I say that the news I was now the Marquess of Lowenbrock came as even more of a surprise to me."

"Well, the tenants couldn't have asked for someone better. I'm sure it's obvious to everyone who meets you that you aren't the type to take advantage of your new wealth to their disadvantage."

"Stop, I'm blushing."

His tone was even, as was his color, and Amelia couldn't help the surprised laugh that burst forth. When heat began to color his cheeks at her reaction, her laughter grew less ladylike. It took about ten seconds before he was laughing as well.

"If my friends were here, they'd never let me hear the end of this. You have to promise you won't tell them about having made me blush when they arrive for the ball." His lips twisted slightly on the last word.

Amelia pressed her lips together and mimed the action of closing a lock.

"Thank you," he said with a dip of his head. His mouth quirked in amusement. "For some reason, the weather has been abysmally cold this summer. Most of the tenants are worried about their crops failing. To ease their worries, Jeffers suggested a summer fair. Something to improve their moods, even if only temporarily." He gave a casual shrug. "It didn't take much to convince me. I've been to my share of country festivals in my youth and find that I've missed them. If anyone deserves some time to enjoy themselves, it would be the families who toil so hard."

Amelia was grinning when he finished. "Do you plan to attend?"

He nodded. "And I hoped you would accompany me. If you wouldn't mind, that is."

"If I wouldn't mind?" Did this man know nothing about women? "I would love to!"

"I'm relieved to hear you say that. I'm finding it difficult to remember everyone's name. I still can't believe so many people are dependent on my decisions."

"Mr. Jeffers took good care of the estate when Uncle passed away, but there was much that fell by the wayside over the past few years." At Lowenbrock's frown, she rushed to add, "He wasn't neglecting his duties. But Uncle was always very generous. We had no way of knowing what the next marquess would see as a frivolous expense, so he was careful not to spend more than was necessary."

Lowenbrock was silent for a moment before giving a sharp nod. "The man admitted as much to me himself. But it bothers me to hear about people living in poverty."

"They were taken care of, as I'm sure you already know. But the estate didn't provide for too many extras. At any rate, you're here now and things will return to normal."

"Or as normal as possible with a marquess who has no idea what he's doing."

Amelia wanted to protest, but she let the comment go. She'd heard horror stories about nobles running their estates into the ground with gambling debts and excessive spending. She'd seen no sign of either inclination from Lowenbrock. Still, he was clearly feeling overwhelmed by his new responsibilities.

"I think a fair is just what everyone needs. You and me included. When is it to be?"

"Jeffers suggested one week from Saturday. That will give the tenants some time to prepare."

"And then the ball is next month."

Lowenbrock let out an exaggerated sigh that had her laughing again.

"Your sisters have replied. They'll be here before the ball with their husbands but felt the trip would be of too short a duration to bring your nieces and nephews. Your friends will be arriving before them, as will my friend Mary."

"You can invite anyone you wish. Lord knows we have more than enough room for guests."

She lifted her shoulder in a slight shrug. "Mary Trenton is my closest friend. And trust me when I say that we will not be lacking for guests."

Lowenbrock took her statement at face value, and she released a soft breath. She wouldn't share the fact that Mary was the only one of her acquaintances she trusted around him. Most of them were already married, but she knew that at least one of them, possibly two, would go out of their way to steal his attention for themselves, and that thought bothered her more than a little. There were already a few beautiful, unattached women from the neighborhood who would do whatever it took to attract his attention.

As they finished the rest of their dessert, she told herself her concern stemmed from practicality. When Lowenbrock wed, it was likely his wife would want her to leave Brock Manor. But she was beginning to realize that she thought of Lowenbrock as belonging to her... She'd even had a dream or two where he'd professed his undying devotion to her.

She couldn't be sure if these feelings were real or if they were wrapped up in the fiction she was writing. She never should have continued with the hero she'd conceived in London when she realized she'd be living under the same room as the man who'd inspired him. The two were muddled in her mind, and while she'd welcome his attention, it was clear that Lowenbrock had no romantic feelings for her.

She excused herself after they finished dinner and returned to her bedroom, her feelings unsettled as she thought about the future. She couldn't help but believe that everything would change after the ball.

CHAPTER 16

THE MORNING OF THE FESTIVAL ARRIVED, the day overcast and cool even for England. At least it wasn't raining, John told himself as he waited in the drawing room for Miss Weston. She had arranged for the staff to bring a light meal to their rooms that morning, so he hadn't seen her yet. He hadn't realized how much he would miss seeing her across the breakfast table from him.

John shifted his shoulders under the tailcoat his valet had chosen for him that morning. Normally he chafed under the formal attire he was expected to wear at all times, but he was glad of it that morning. The thick wool of the dark brown garment should be enough to keep him warm. He wondered if Amelia would have to wear a cloak. She would catch a chill if she wore one of her morning gowns.

He glanced toward the doorway, wondering how

much longer he'd have to wait. As though he'd conjured her from his thoughts, he found her entering the room. He rose swiftly to his feet and couldn't keep himself from staring at her for several seconds.

He'd always thought she was pretty even with her hair covered and when she wore her spectacles. But in that moment he became painfully aware of the truth. Amelia Weston had been hiding her beauty.

In the time since they'd met, he'd come to know her spirit and liked her as a person. He told himself that he considered her a friend. It was evident though that his feelings for her went far beyond mere friend-ship. Much as he had tried since coming to live at Brock Manor, he could no longer deny that he was attracted to her.

It had been several weeks since he'd last seen her wearing her glasses. He assumed she only needed them while writing or doing close work. This was the first time, however, that he'd seen her without a lace cap covering her hair.

He'd known that her hair was dark, but seeing it uncovered lent an air of intimacy to their interactions that was unexpected. She wore the dark mass pinned up, of course, but a few curls had been left loose to frame her face. Still, it was a formal style. Seeing her in the deep blue dress that matched her eye color and complemented her light skin tone—far different from the pale dresses she normally wore—he became aware of her in a way that made him more than a little uncomfortable.

That was especially true when he realized he hadn't been wrong in thinking the woman standing before him now bore a striking resemblance to the one he'd met in the tavern in London, the barmaid who'd captured his attention when he'd first laid eyes on her.

He looked away for a moment to clear his head. Yes, Amelia was similar in appearance to the barmaid Molly, but that could only be a coincidence. He'd thought his memory of that night remained clear, but somewhere along the way he'd superimposed Amelia's features onto that of the other woman. After all, Amelia had been here in Yorkshire that night, and she didn't have any sisters.

"I apologize for keeping you waiting. It's been so long since I've been to a fair, and I fear vanity had me taking longer than normal this morning."

He dipped his head in a formal bow. "It was more than worth the wait." A light color tinged her cheeks at his compliment, and John couldn't hold back his smile. He did love teasing her, but his next words were entirely truthful. "You look beautiful, Miss Weston. I hope you won't be too cold, however."

She leaned toward him and he found himself watching her expression with great care, wondering at the way her eyes had lit with amusement.

"I'm wearing a few extra layers under my skirts. I should be warm enough once I don my spencer."

And just like that, he found himself imagining what was under her skirts. For one insane moment, he wondered if that had been her intent. Fortunately, he was saved from embarrassing himself when she turned to leave the room. He fell into step beside her and watched as the butler helped her into the short navy blue coat that would cover her arms and breasts.

Good heavens, he was in a bad way. He had to stop thinking about the barmaid who'd awoken his desires that evening that seemed so long ago. If he could behave honorably around a woman who'd been in danger of falling out of her dress, he could do the same for this woman who was nothing but circumspect in her behavior and appearance.

He clutched his hands behind his back to keep from taking the garment from Hastings and helping her into it himself. He forced himself to look away while she did up the buttons. She took her gloves from Hastings with a soft thank-you and turned to face him with a wide smile.

"I am ready to brave what has to be the coolest summer in history."

Her amusement was infectious. He held out his arm for her to take, and together they left the house. "With any luck, the sun will come out at some point."

She gave her head a small shake, drawing his attention to the way the curls danced around her face.

"Let's not be greedy. I will be content if it doesn't rain."

He chuckled as he led her to the carriage that waited outside. It felt unnatural to wait for a footman to open the door for them, but he forced himself to do just that. He did, however, perform the task of helping Amelia into the carriage himself. He sprang in after her and closed the door behind them.

The carriage ride was short. When they arrived, the festivities were already underway. From the large groups of people milling around the various stalls, it was clear that many people from the nearby village were also in attendance.

John helped Amelia down from the carriage. He'd already given the staff permission to attend the festival, and now he did the same for the coachman and the young footman who'd accompanied them.

When he turned back to Amelia, his arm already raised for her to take, he found her examining him. The corners of her mouth had turned up in a small smile, her eyes warm with approval at what she no doubt perceived as his generosity. But it hadn't been that long since John was a young man without money or a future. He wouldn't deny others the small enjoyments they could gain when the opportunity presented itself.

She slipped her hand into the bend of his elbow, and he gazed down at her. He wanted to ask her why such a small gesture would gain her approval when, by all accounts, her uncle had also been a generous man.

Instead, he asked, "What shall we do first, my lady?"

When her gaze swung to take in the stalls and the merriment that surrounded them, he took a moment to examine her again. The corners of her eyes crinkled with her smile, joy radiating from her.

He tore his gaze away lest he be caught staring and took in the scene. Given just how little time they'd had to organize this event, he was impressed by the number of stalls and tables set up. He wouldn't be surprised to learn that everyone in the entire county who had anything to sell was there. Crafts of all types were on display, the tables laden with sweets.

And right in the center of it all, a puppet theater had been set up. Given the small crowd that had gathered before the miniature stage, he expected the show to begin at any moment.

A pang of nostalgia swept through him when he witnessed a group of boys chasing each other and ducking through the stalls.

Amelia made a small noise, and he turned to face her, enjoying the hint of mischief in her expression.

"Do I want to know what you have in mind?"

She laughed, the sound full and rich. "I think we'll start with the puppet show and see where the day takes us."

CHAPTER 17

*A*MELIA WASN'T SURPRISED to see how much everyone liked Lowenbrock. He'd only been in residence for two months, but she knew he'd been busy during that time. And despite his statement to the contrary, he seemed to remember everyone's name. She'd only had to step in twice when she realized he was floundering to put a name to a face. On both occasions, however, they'd been visitors from the neighboring village and not one of the estate's tenants.

What did surprise her was how he made it a point to visit every booth and table that had been set up, buying gifts for his sisters and each member of their families. He'd even sampled something from each of the food stalls, complimenting the women, who were clearly anxious about his opinion on their offerings.

She watched as he took up a bow to join an

archery competition. He wasn't the best archer present, but he more than held his own.

She spotted Mr. Jeffers heading her way and called out a greeting when he reached her. "Where is Mrs. Jeffers today?"

The steward smiled and gave his head a small shake. "She pointed me in this direction, saying she was buying something she doesn't want me to see. My birthday is coming up next month, so…"

He raised one shoulder in a small shrug. The small smile he tried to hide spoke volumes about their relationship. One didn't have to see the two of them together to know the man cared very much for his wife. It was obvious in the way his eyes softened whenever he mentioned her.

"I'll have to look for her later then. I wouldn't want to shirk my duty in keeping you occupied while she does her shopping."

Mr. Jeffers let out a small laugh and turned toward the group participating in the archery competition. After observing for a minute, he said, "I think Lowenbrock is holding back."

"What makes you say that?" Amelia's gaze focused on the marquess, wondering what Mr. Jeffers had seen.

"Something about the way he handles the bow tells me he's had a great deal of experience wielding them."

Amelia narrowed her eyes and watched how he

held the weapon and drew it up to aim. He did seem to know what he was doing. "Perhaps, but that doesn't mean he has good aim."

Silence stretched between them as they watched Lowenbrock let loose an arrow. It landed just a small distance from the center of the ring, but it wasn't closest to the mark. "You think he's trying to ensure he doesn't win?"

"It's possible. There's a cash prize for the winner, and he strikes me as the type of man who wouldn't allow his competitive streak to keep money from a family in need."

Amelia watched as Lowenbrock's rival puffed up with pride and took his place for the next round. She suspected the steward was correct. The marquess wouldn't want to make it too obvious though.

"Given the fact that the crops aren't thriving this year, the marquess has come to a unique understanding about the rents."

Amelia faced the man. "He hasn't said anything to me about it. Should you be sharing this information?"

Mr. Jeffers didn't take his gaze from the marquess when he replied. "It isn't a secret. Everyone knows."

Curiosity overcame her. "They'd hate accepting charity." She crossed her arms and waited for him to divulge the information he so clearly wanted to.

"Yes, His Lordship came to that realization himself. Which is why he met with each family individually. He explained that there were others in need of assistance but who wouldn't want to accept charity. He told them that he plans to keep this year's rents in a separate fund for those whose crops fail to produce as expected."

Amelia shook in wonder. So many would not be so kind. "And if few can contribute to that fund?" But she already knew what the answer would be.

"He'll be financing it himself, of course, to ensure none go without this winter." Mr. Jeffers faced her then. "He's a good man. If your uncle were still alive, he'd be happy to see a match between you."

Amelia looked away, embarrassed by the observation. First Mr. Markham and now Mr. Jeffers was suggesting there should be a match between her and Lowenbrock.

"Yes, well, I imagine every eligible female in the region will feel the same way. And when he meets some of them at the ball, he likely won't even remember my name."

The look he gave her was enigmatic at best. But when his gaze drifted to the side, he broke into the widest grin she'd ever seen from the man. She hadn't known he was capable of expressing so much emotion.

Amelia followed his gaze and wasn't surprised to see his wife approaching. Mrs. Jeffers looked very pretty that morning, tendrils of her light brown hair curling about her face. She was wearing a white cloak that made her look almost like an angel. It was no secret that the steward was truly besotted by his wife, and Amelia had come to learn that the woman felt the same way about her husband.

She was carrying a wrapped package. When Mr. Jeffers reached out to take it from her, she shifted to the side and gave her head a firm shake.

"You won't discover what I bought that easily. You'll have to wait until your birthday."

Mr. Jeffers raised one brow, which had the result of causing his wife to huff out a small breath.

"Take note, Miss Weston, that husbands are often like little boys. Don't be surprised if yours goes searching through the house to find out what you got him for his birthday."

Mr. Jeffers chuckled. "My wife exaggerates. It isn't my fault she leaves her packages lying about for anyone to find."

Amelia laughed at the light banter between the two. They bid her goodbye, and she watched as they walked away. Despite her protestations, Mrs. Jeffers allowed her husband to take the package she'd been carrying and took his arm. She leaned into him as they strolled toward a table where some sweetmeats were laid out.

The way they smiled at each other caused a pang within Amelia's heart. She wanted what they had for herself, but she'd have to be content to write about it instead.

Her gaze drifted back to Lowenbrock. She'd

missed the end of the contest. He murmured something to the man with whom he'd been competing.
From the way he clapped the other man on the back,
it was clear Lowenbrock hadn't won. She wouldn't be
surprised to learn the steward had been correct in his
assessment of the marquess's abilities with a bow.

When his gaze met hers across the field, he smiled
and headed toward her. A small zing of anticipation
unfurled in Amelia's belly, one she tried her best to
ignore. They were friends, nothing more. It was
normal to be happy to see one's friends.

She ignored the little voice that reminded her
she'd never felt this way about anyone else.

Lowenbrock's step faltered, and he turned to greet
a woman who had placed a hand on his arm. A
woman whose attire revealed far too much flesh given
the weather. The petite woman fluttered her lashes at
Lowenbrock and leaned forward slightly so he
wouldn't be able to avoid seeing right down the front
of her dress.

She must have been a new resident of the village,
or perhaps a visitor from farther away, because
Amelia didn't recognize her. As she watched the
marquess smile down at the woman, Amelia was
powerless to stop the anger that swept through her.

She tore her gaze from them and spun around to
look at something—anything—else. Her gaze settled
on a little girl who was trying to drag her mother
toward one of the games that had been set up. With a

sigh, the woman gave in and allowed her daughter to lead her in that direction.

Normally the sight would have brought a smile to Amelia's face, but she couldn't forget the way Lowenbrock had smiled down at that woman. And the way she'd leaned in just a little too close in response.

Amelia had been wrong to think she could only be friends with this man. From the moment he'd rescued her in London, she'd done everything in her power to deny her attraction to him. She'd tried to convince herself that her fascination with everything he did and the way he looked, so effortlessly handsome, was only her desire to study him so she could base her hero on him. Lowenbrock and the hero of her book had diverged at some point because it had felt more than a little uncomfortable to continue to base her hero on the man with whom she lived so closely. But her fascination with him hadn't waned. Quite the contrary, it had only grown with each passing day.

She cast her gaze around, looking for something to do so she could escape her thoughts. When she heard a throat clear right behind her, she actually jumped. She turned to find Lowenbrock standing there. Her gaze moved behind him and she spotted the other woman glaring at them, her expression thunderous.

Amelia could not hold back her relief as she greeted the marquess. She took the arm he offered, and they began another sweep of the fairgrounds.

Looking up at him, she said, "You acquitted yourself well."

His expression didn't change. "Not well enough to win."

She made a sound that could be taken for agreement. "I saw Mr. Jeffers."

Lowenbrock met her gaze and looked away. "He did say he planned to attend."

Amelia leaned a little closer, making sure to keep her voice low. "He believes you purposely lost the competition."

"Does he now?"

Amelia examined his expression. This was a man who would not easily give up his secrets. "Did you?"

One small corner of his mouth lifted, but he didn't reply.

Amelia took that as assent and her already high estimation of his character rose even higher.

CHAPTER 18

*A*s the day progressed, they were accosted several times by young women hoping to catch Lowenbrock's eye. Not one of them would be socially acceptable as a match for the marquess, but that didn't stop them from propositioning him.

Not outright, of course. Not with her standing right beside him most of the time. But it was clear they were hoping he'd spend time with them. There were even a few married women who tried their luck.

Amelia supposed she should count herself lucky that the eligible women had quit the area for London. But those whose search for a husband on the marriage mart proved fruitless would return even more determined to ensnare the marquess for themselves. When they arrived at the ball and saw for themselves just how handsome he was, they would be relentless. And when Lowenbrock wed, her time at Brock Manor would come to an end. Not because Lowenbrock would ask her to leave. And it was possible that whomever he wed wouldn't take issue with her remaining in residence.

No, watching all those women trying to capture the marquess's eye made her realize she couldn't live under the same roof with Lowenbrock and his future wife. Not when it was clear she couldn't see him with another woman without experiencing the irrational sting of jealousy.

It was obvious to her that she had come to care for this man as more than just a friend. It was possible she was already falling in love with him. It was also clear, from his circumspect behavior toward her, that he didn't return the sentiment.

Or at least she didn't think he did. She couldn't but help wonder if he was hiding his feelings. If there was one thing she knew about the marquess, it was that he would never take advantage of someone he considered one of his charges. He was generous enough to lose a competition on purpose if that person needed the prize money, and he'd done so in a manner that wouldn't wound the man's pride. It was entirely possible he would go out of his way to hide any attraction he might feel toward her.

Not likely, but possible.

By the time he helped her up into the carriage for their return trip home, a terrible idea had taken shape. She tried to push it aside, engaging in small talk with Lowenbrock to distract herself, but it was no use. She couldn't ignore the way his smile made her heart flutter. And the way his eyes crinkled in the corners with genuine amusement as he recounted an amusing tale about his nieces and nephews only served to increase just how attractive she found this man.

When the carriage pulled up in front of the house, she sympathized with all those women who had thrown themselves at him. And she'd come to the decision that she was going to do the same thing.

She hadn't even realized she'd become quiet as she tried to imagine how to go about accomplishing it. She'd seen all manner of approaches that day. What would it be like to bask in this man's attention for a brief time?

She hesitated when Lowenbrock stepped down from the carriage and held his hand out to her.

Now that she'd come to the decision that she wanted this man to teach her about the intimacy that could be found between a man and a woman, every interaction between them took on a new significance. The simple act of placing her hand on his arm as he led her into the house—something she'd done numerous times that day as they strolled through the fair—left her feeling tongue-tied. She said nothing as Hastings opened the door for them and took her spencer and gloves. It was around the time they normally took their dinner, but given how much food they'd sampled throughout the day, neither of them were hungry.

Deep in thought, she wandered into the drawing room and took a seat on the settee.

Normally Lowenbrock sat in one of the chairs, but today he chose to sit next to her, and given her new awareness of the man, her thoughts all but scattered.

"What are you thinking that has you so quiet? It seems as though you're carrying the weight of the world on your shoulders."

Amelia glanced at him and took in the way his forehead had wrinkled. She vacillated for a moment before squaring her shoulders. She was no longer a young girl. If all those other women could do this, so could she.

"I couldn't help but notice all the attention you attracted today."

His brows drew together. "That was to be expected. While I still find it difficult to believe I've inherited all this…" He waved his hand to indicate the house and everything that came along with it, then lifted one shoulder in a shrug. "I've met most of the tenants, but they're still curious about me. And there were many there today who'd never met me before. I'm not sure why that would surprise you."

Amelia summoned all the bravery she'd needed the night she'd dressed so provocatively and pretended to be the barmaid Molly. "There were more than a few women who seemed to want to get to know you better."

The way the tips of his ears turned red told her that he'd realized just what those women were doing. "I apologize if that made you uncomfortable."

She resisted the urge to place a hand on his arm. The instinct to comfort him was almost overwhelming, but she couldn't be that forward. "I wasn't so much uncomfortable as I was… angry."

His head tilted to one side, his eyes widening in surprise, but he waited for her to continue.

"Well, not angry exactly." She let out a small breath of annoyance when she found herself hesitating. "I came to realize that their attention caused me no small amount of jealousy because I wanted your attention for myself."

CHAPTER 19

*H*E HADN'T HEARD HER CORRECTLY. He'd spent a great deal of time that day reining in his inappropriate thoughts, wishing that one of the not-so-subtle propositions he'd received had come from this very woman. And now he was misinterpreting her statement. Or worse, imagining her words.

Conscious of just how close they sat, he had to force his thoughts away from leaning closer, stealing a kiss. "You were jealous?"

She looked away for a moment before nodding.

"Because…?"

She kept her gaze averted, and he allowed his eyes to trace along the line of her slender throat. Her hair was still bound, and his thoughts turned to snagging the pins that kept it up and watching as the mass tumbled down around her shoulders. And damn him if it didn't occur to him again just how much Amelia reminded him of the barmaid Molly.

But despite that stray thought, it was painfully evident to him how much he wanted *this* woman.

"It was difficult enough to admit the first time."

He wasn't about to make assumptions, not about this. "I must insist. This is too important a subject for misunderstandings."

She fidgeted, twining her fingers together in her lap. Her reticence had him thinking that perhaps he wasn't losing his mind as he'd feared.

She took a deep breath and met his gaze. "You know my age."

"You are five and twenty."

She nodded. "Well and truly on the shelf."

The pieces of a puzzle were beginning to form in his mind. Still, he wasn't about to leap to conclusions.

She closed her eyes for a moment, and John assumed she'd decided against continuing with their conversation. He could only imagine how difficult it had been for her to reveal as much as she already had. Still, he couldn't allow his attraction to Amelia to sway his actions. Before anything could happen between them, he had to know that she wanted him as much as he wanted her.

She straightened her shoulders and met his gaze again. "I am old enough now to know my own mind. I know that I might never have a husband and children, but that doesn't mean I can't know the physical side of what happens between a man and a woman."

His heart rate increased, and a haze of lust threatened to rob him of his senses. It took an immeasurable amount of willpower not to take her into his arms. "Are you actually asking me...?" He couldn't finish the question. He wanted this too much, and he wouldn't dishonor her by forcing his attentions on her. Amelia, with her avid curiosity, could very well be asking him to share his experiences with her. She was a writer, after all, and perhaps she just wanted to know details about the physical side of love.

Her gaze didn't waver from his. "I would like you to make love to me."

Blood pounded in his ears, and for a moment he was incapable of thought or speech.

"Please don't make me ask again."

He didn't know what to say. His first instinct was to grab hold of her and give her what he'd never imagined she wanted. Show her how good it could be between a man and a woman. Not that he actually knew himself. His own experiences had been brief encounters, and more than a few of them had ended with the exchange of coin. Still, he knew there was more to it than the quick rutting that constituted most of his experience. He wanted to explore that side of lovemaking with her so much he ached. He would be slow and careful—

Amelia looked away and stood. He followed automatically, confused when she stumbled backward.

"Please, forget I said anything. It's clear you don't think of me that way."

He laughed, a short staccato burst of sound. He had no words for how ridiculous he found her statement. She took it the wrong way, however, and turned to flee from the room.

She had to run past him, however, and he took hold of her arm before she could escape.

"You don't have to laugh at me. You could have just said no. Made one of those polite excuses you no doubt used when all those other women propositioned you."

"Stop, Amelia."

Her eyes widened, and she ceased trying to pull away. Her name on his tongue had surprised her.

He released her arm. "I am not laughing at you."

She crossed her arms beneath her chest, and it took all his strength not to follow the movement when the action served to push up her breasts.

"It sounded like a laugh to me."

He smiled. She was adorable in her anger. How could she believe he thought her request ridiculous?

"I laughed because I'd imagined being with you many times, especially today when you stopped hiding from me. But I'd convinced myself it wasn't possible."

His admission served to ease some of her anger, but he didn't think she believed him.

"Because you don't think of me that way?"

He shook his head. "I just told you that I do think of you in that way... often."

She took a deep breath, and this time he couldn't stop himself from glancing down to the enhanced display of her charms before he dragged his gaze back up to her face.

"Does that mean you'll...?"

When she took another deep breath, he couldn't help but wonder if she was trying to kill him.

"What it means is that I would like nothing more than to satisfy your curiosity." He almost groaned aloud at his horrible choice of words. "But we both know it isn't possible. I'm your protector, and I won't use you in such a manner."

But he could marry her.

CHAPTER 20

*H*IS REFUSAL THREATENED her ability to breathe.

Lowenbrock had admitted he imagined being with her. It shouldn't have surprised her, yet it did. From everything she'd read and witnessed with her own eyes, men were freer when it came to casual lovemaking. But Lowenbrock clearly wasn't as taken with her as she'd hoped. She was a fool. The attraction she felt for him was one-sided and he was being polite to spare her feelings.

Her humiliation was complete. "I understand," she said, trying to gather the shredded remains of her dignity.

She started to turn away, knowing he wouldn't stop her from leaving a second time, but she was mistaken. He moved so quickly she was in his arms before she realized what was happening. Her body was scant inches away from his, and she could feel the heat of his body reaching out for her.

"Do you know how lovemaking works, Amelia?"

She could only nod, unable to form words. She'd been naive once, but one young woman who lived in the village had taken delight in shocking Amelia with her knowledge after she'd wed.

"Do you know what happens to a man's body when he aches to make love to a woman?"

She'd been mistaken when she thought she'd already reached the depths of her humiliation. "I understand what you're saying. You don't think you can… perform." Surely she would never be able to face his man again.

He tugged her against him, her entire body pressing against his.

"Can you feel that? Do you know what it means?"

Her mouth went dry as she took in his meaning. She'd noticed how muscular he was, but what she felt pressed into her lower belly was not muscle. It was his manhood. Which meant he did find her desirable. That he wanted to make love to her.

She wanted to say something witty and worldly, but all her bravado had been used up when she asked him to make love to her. So instead of replying with words, she nodded.

"Make no mistake, I would like nothing more than to take you upstairs right now and give you *every-thing* you want."

She licked her lips, and he let out a small groan, lowering his head so his face was scant inches from hers.

"Can I kiss you, Miss Weston?"

It was ridiculous. He'd already called her by her given name, so why did she feel a little thrill now that he was being so formal? She'd examine that emotion later. For now, she wanted this moment to continue, afraid that any delay on her part would lead to Lowenbrock changing his mind.

"Yes," she said, her voice barely above a whisper.

She held her breath until he covered her mouth with his, and then she released it with a soft sigh. She'd never kissed a man before. It was a gentle touch, his mouth against hers, but she felt the shock of the intimacy through her entire body.

She leaned closer into him, enjoying the way he cradled her face with his hands. His lips moved against hers, deepening slightly and then retreating. Each time he started to draw back, she followed him, wanting nothing more than for their kiss to continue forever.

She grasped his shoulders, fearing he would end this too-perfect moment before she was ready. But then he did something she wasn't expecting. He touched her lips with his tongue.

Instinct took over, and she didn't realize she'd opened her mouth until he deepened the kiss, exploring her mouth. She wanted to get closer to this man, wanted to crawl into his skin. Since that wasn't possible, she answered his exploration with her own.

She made a soft sound of pleasure. When he drew back, she opened her eyes to find him staring down at her. She waited in silence, her heart pounding in her ears.

"Stopping right now is going to be one of the most difficult things I've ever done." There was a roughness to his voice that underscored his words.

Disappointment threatened to overwhelm her. "Then don't stop."

There was something about his expression, a hunger in his gaze, that had her convinced he was about to acquiesce.

"I need to ask you something, Amelia."

She nodded. He took it as permission to question her, but she was already giving him her answer. Yes, she wanted him to make love to her.

"Will you consent to be my wife?"

She opened her mouth to say yes but then froze when she realized what he'd asked her. Her heart screamed at her to accept his proposal, but her logical nature chose that moment to assert itself.

"Why?" she asked.

Her question caught him off guard. Well, good. Turnabout was fair play, after all.

"Why should you marry me?"

She shook her head. "No. I want to know why you're proposing marriage."

He didn't even hesitate. "So that I can take care of you."

She waited a few seconds, but it became clear he wasn't going to elaborate. She pushed against his shoulders and he released her immediately.

"That's why you want to marry me? So you can take care of me?"

"Well, yes. That and the fact we're clearly attracted to one another."

She shouldn't ask her next question. She knew it would lead to heartbreak, yet she couldn't seem to stop herself. "Do you love me?"

This time he did hesitate, and her fragile elation at being held in this man's arms disappeared.

"I don't know. I like you a great deal, and I want to take care of you. It's almost a compulsion at this point."

She thought back to the way he'd stepped in that night at the tavern and helped her when things got out of hand with one of the patrons. She couldn't help but wonder if he made rescuing women his mission in life. Much as she wanted to accept his proposal, she needed to be more to him than an obligation. "I am not a child, my lord."

He frowned at her use of the honorific but didn't correct her. "Of course not. Our embrace is evidence I don't think of you that way."

He'd admitted that he cared for her as a friend. She shouldn't be so fixated on words, but it seemed she needed them. Perhaps if she didn't love him, it would be enough to accept what he was offering her. It was more than many women had when they accepted an offer of marriage or when their families arranged one for them. It would seem, however, that she wasn't content to accept a practical union from Lowenbrock. It would hurt too much. She wanted everything from him.

She wouldn't deny him. Instead, she'd wait. Give him time to learn whether he could come to love her as much as she loved him.

She forced herself to smile at him, hoping he wouldn't see her sorrow. "Perhaps you should ask me again at a different time. If you don't change your mind, that is."

His brows lowered into a confused frown. "You're denying me?"

"No, I'm not. I'm saying that we should postpone this conversation for a later time."

He didn't withdraw from her physically, but she could almost feel the emotional wall he placed between them. "As you wish."

"My earlier statement is still true. I would welcome you into my bed tonight."

She saw the flicker of yearning in his eyes before he looked away and gave his head a sharp shake.

She sighed. This man was one of the most stubborn people she'd ever met. But that mattered not, because he'd met his match in her. He *would* make love to her. She knew with certainty now that he wasn't immune to her. He did want her as a man wanted a woman. Only time would tell if he could come to think of her as more than a friend, as more than someone he felt obliged to care for.

She would give him that time. Until then, she'd make him understand that he didn't need to marry her for them to be together.

CHAPTER 21

*J*OHN TOSSED AND TURNED in his large, empty bed. As the hours crept by, he found it more difficult to understand why he'd thought it better to sleep alone.

He didn't regret asking Amelia to marry him. He was confident they'd be good together in every way, not just in the bedroom. But as the clock chimed each hour, he started to convince himself that perhaps the road to wooing the stubborn Amelia Weston lay in giving her what they both wanted.

When he finally managed to fall asleep, nightmarish recollections of battles past woke him early the next morning. Giving up on sleep, he dressed and went for his customary morning ride. He'd hoped the exercise and morning air would clear his head, but when he returned to the stables, he was still conflicted about his future course of action.

Normally he made his way to the breakfast room where Amelia would be waiting for him, but he suspected she would need just as much time and space to think as he. He asked a footman to arrange for a tray to be brought to his study and headed there instead.

What he didn't expect was to find her waiting for him in his study. She was seated at his desk, and it took him a moment to realize she was going over the estate's account book. Jeffers must have updated them, and they made it a habit of going over the figures together.

He drank in the sight of her. Her dark hair was pulled back, not one curl framing her face as it had the day before. He was glad to see that she hadn't gone back to wearing her lace cap. But her spectacles were perched on her nose as she read.

She glanced up when she realized she was no longer alone. The wide smile that spread across her face had him answering in kind.

She rose and moved around the desk, stopping before him. "I wasn't sure I was going to see you today," she said, dipping into a deep curtsy.

He almost swore when he saw that the dress she wore was designed to show more of her décolletage than the ones she normally wore when at home. It didn't take much imagination to guess what her breasts would look like because they almost spilled over the top of her dress. And the way she stayed in the curtsy for several long moments...

He wanted to swear. "What are you doing, Amelia?"

She looked up at him but didn't rise. The mischief in her eyes had him wanting to groan. Clearly she hadn't given up on her scheme to seduce him. If anything, she seemed more determined than ever.

Ever so slowly, she straightened. "I'm attempting to change your mind. Is it working?"

If she lowered her gaze, she'd see just how well it was working. "Yes, it is."

A hint of elation lit her eyes when he took a step closer, but it disappeared when he moved past her and put the desk between them. She pouted at the large piece of furniture that now separated them.

"Is there anything I need to know about the accounts?"

She shook her head, defeat evident in her posture. "Everything appears to be running smoothly."

They stared at one another for several seconds, and John came to a decision. If Amelia wanted seduction, he'd give it to her. But once he started on that path, he wasn't sure he'd be able to stop himself from taking her to bed before she accepted his offer of marriage.

He reached out to her. Her mouth turned up again with a cautious smile as she rounded the desk and placed her hand in his. Neither of them were wearing gloves, and warmth unfurled in his chest as he engulfed her smaller hand in his.

"One kiss," he said.

He didn't mind the look of triumph that crossed her face. They were both getting what they wanted in that moment.

"I'm content to start with that, my lord." She dipped into another curtsy but kept her hand in his. Once again, he was presented with a generous display of her breasts.

With a mock growl of annoyance, he pulled her closer, enjoying the laugh that escaped her. "I see you're intent on testing my restraint."

"Restraint is vastly overrated."

She rose onto her toes, slipped her hand from his, and grasped his shoulders. He settled on holding her by the waist, telling himself he wouldn't stray from that spot.

This time there was no tentative press of his mouth against hers. Even if he'd wanted to go slowly, she opened her mouth under his and stole all his senses.

Her hands were in his hair, her body pressed tightly against his. Her low moan of contentment had him groaning in response.

This had been a tactical error on his part. He wasn't going to be able to resist her for long if he allowed her to continue to get under his skin in this manner.

To his surprise, she pulled away first. One of her hands moved to his chest, where she flattened it over his racing heart. He longed to do the same to her, but if he touched her breasts, he would have her right there on the desk. And he wanted to make sure their first time together wasn't a rushed affair. She deserved a comfortable bed and seduction.

She hasn't agreed to marry you yet.

But even as the thought rose to the surface of his muddled brain, he realized he'd already lost this battle. He wouldn't be able to wait for her to agree to his proposal. He wondered whether he could induce her to accept him after they made love.

She wet her lips, and the sight of her tongue peeking out for that small moment had him hardening even further.

"Perhaps later tonight…"

She didn't need to finish the statement. She was clearly an innocent if she thought she needed to wait for night to fall before making love to a man. He grasped onto her invitation to delay their current activity, needing to get his jumbled thoughts under control. It probably wouldn't help, but he didn't want to scare her away with just how much he wanted her. There would be other times to show her the different times of day—and places—they could make love.

He nodded and forced his fingers to release their grasp of her waist. Her smile this time wasn't one of triumph but what he hoped was genuine affection. He watched her as she turned and left the room, his eyes glued to her backside under the voluminous folds of her skirt. Soon enough he'd know what it felt like to hold that part of her in his hands. Amelia had asked him to make love to her, and he would give her exactly what she wanted.

And then he'd make her see just how much they were suited and she'd agree to marry him.

CHAPTER 22

THE DAY DRAGGED ON, and it seemed as though dinner would never arrive. Somehow John managed to force his attention on the accounts after Amelia left. But his thoughts kept drifting back to her, anticipation tightening within him as he looked forward to their night together.

The only thing that kept his mind on the task at hand was the knowledge that his steward would be arriving at eleven, as was his custom when he updated the account books. The man's serious demeanor kept John's thoughts from drifting back to Amelia and the way she'd felt in his arms.

Finally it was time to join Amelia for dinner. He entered the drawing room earlier than normal. Unable to release the tension that coiled through his body, he paced as he waited for her arrival.

When he turned for what felt like the hundredth

time, he spotted her standing just inside the threshold. Her dress was a pale lavender, a color that accentuated her fair skin and dark hair. And her blue eyes shone with a glow that had him aching to take her into his arms again.

When he spotted the footman hovering in the hallway, he had to settle for a smile and a murmured greeting. As they'd done every evening, she took his arm and together they made their way to the dining room. He was grinning like a fool.

Instead of allowing a footman to draw out her chair, he performed the task himself, barely restraining the urge to caress the skin of her neck. He made his way to the opposite side of the table and waited as the footman served the soup dish.

"You appear to be in a good mood, my lord."

He realized he'd been imagining how she'd look rounded with his child and gave his head a small shake to clear his thoughts. He needed to ensure that didn't happen until after they wed.

"How could I be anything else when I'm having dinner with the most beautiful woman in all of England?"

Their eyes met and held before she looked away. She wasn't afflicted with his own curse of blushing when embarrassed, but he knew his words had affected her.

"I can't believe this is happening," she said, her

voice pitched low so the footman wouldn't overhear their conversation.

"If we wait a little while longer, my family will be here to properly chaperone us." He was teasing, of course. He knew she wanted this as much as he did. Still, he felt the need to give her an excuse to back out if she'd changed her mind.

"Don't you dare." The glare she sent him was teasing, but he knew she was serious.

Dinner seemed to take twice as long as normal. The glances she cast his way had him hard for most of the meal. He only survived without betraying himself to the staff because she wasn't sitting close enough for him to touch her. But if he was being honest, he didn't care if the whole world knew they would soon be together.

No matter how much care they took, there would be gossip belowstairs. Instead of dragging her into his arms when the meal was over, he inclined his head when she bid him good night. He waited for her to leave the dining room first, averting his gaze instead of watching the way her backside swayed slightly, and then made his way to his own chambers after a respectable amount of time had passed.

He waited an hour before leaving his rooms again. He'd wanted to go to her directly, but he had to allow enough time for her maid to help her prepare for bed. He'd dismissed his own valet after he'd appeared in his room.

It was a ritual they went through every night. Oliver would appear, offer his assistance, and John would dismiss him. Maybe one day he'd grow used to the custom, but for now he wasn't comfortable standing there while another man dressed and undressed him.

It was enough for the older man that John made a point of laying his clothes out neatly in his dressing room for his valet to arrange to have cleaned or put away.

John had removed his cravat, but he still wore his waistcoat as he made his way to Amelia's bedroom. He rarely wore a formal topcoat when home, so his appearance wouldn't cause any raised eyebrows if he ran into one of the staff.

He tapped on her door, and it opened a crack. Amelia peeked out at him. He was about to ask if she was alone, but the way she opened the door wide and pulled him into the room was all the answer he needed.

He waited for her to lock the door and turn to face him again. She wore a linen nightdress that should have been proper, but on her was sin itself. Instead of the extra volume of fabric that draped from the bodices of the dresses she wore every day, the fabric fell in a straight line from her shoulder to the floor. And since Amelia's figure was anything but straight, the fabric clung to her breasts and hips, accentuating her body in ways he realized he'd seen once before. Her hair spilled down around her shoulders in dark waves that he longed to bury his fingers in.

He stood in shocked silence for several seconds but decided to wait until later to ask her why she'd tried to hide the fact they'd already met. He had other matters to attend to first.

"I take it you're alone?"

She huffed out a surprised laugh. "I've been alone for the past forty-five minutes. I feigned a headache and told my maid I was going straight to bed."

She moved into his arms and tilted her face up. He needed no further inducement to take the kiss she offered. The one he'd been craving all day since she left his study.

CHAPTER 23

*H*E WAS FINALLY KISSING HER. Dinner had been fraught with tension on her part, and she'd half convinced herself something would happen to prevent Lowenbrock from visiting her as he'd promised. It seemed too much to hope for.

She'd made sure to dismiss her maid quickly and settled in to wait. And wait.

Finally the discreet knock at her door came. And now he was here, and heavens, the man could make a woman weep with the way he kissed.

A shiver went through her when he raised his head and pressed his mouth to the side of her throat. She tilted her head to the side, giving him unrestricted access. His hands moved from her waist to settle on her hips, bringing her flush against the ridge of his arousal. She was slightly shocked by the moan that escaped her throat, a sound that could only be described as wanton.

He lifted his head to look down at her, a wicked smile on his lips. Good Lord, this man was going to be the death of her. If she weren't looking forward to this so much, she would be drowning in embarrassment.

"You should go lie down on the bed. It seems I have a bit of undressing to do to catch up with you."

She almost told him she would help but decided to save that for another time. For now, she'd be content to watch him disrobe, a thought which enthralled her more than it should.

The bedsheets were already turned down, but she decided to sit on the edge of the bed instead of lying down as he'd suggested. In that moment, she was acutely aware of her inexperience.

His eyes remained on her as he undid the buttons of his waistcoat and removed the garment. It said a lot about him that he didn't throw the garment on the floor but instead folded it and turned to drape it over the bench at her dressing table. He remained facing away as he tugged the shirt from his trousers and pulled the white lawn garment over his head.

Her mouth went dry as she took in the muscles of his broad shoulders. She'd known he was strong, she'd felt as much for herself when he'd held her in his arms. But watching the way his muscles rippled as he moved was another thing altogether.

And then he turned around. Her mouth dropped

open as her eyes eagerly took him in. The broad muscles of his arms and shoulders, his chest, and then his abdomen. Good heavens, were all men built in this way? The ridges of muscles, the fair hair that covered him, trailing down to a line that disappeared beneath the trousers he still wore.

He seemed content to stand still and allow her to look her fill. When she realized she'd been staring for far too long, she closed her mouth with a snap and gave her head a small shake.

She wanted to say something witty to break the tension, but her throat had gone dry. She didn't think she would survive if she had to sit there and watch him remove the rest of his clothing.

Either he realized that fact or he wanted to touch her as much as she did him because he crossed the short distance that separated them and sat next to her on the bed.

His voice was rough when he spoke. "You must tell me if I do anything you're uncomfortable with. I want to take my time and go slow with you, but I'm not sure I'll be able to manage it. But if you tell me to stop, I will."

Was there another man alive who would make such an offer? The man who'd shown an interest in her that night at the tavern had seemed intent on taking what he wanted without her permission.

There was so much of Lowenbrock's skin on display, but she wasn't brave enough to touch him yet.

She settled for placing a hand over the fabric that encased his thigh.

"I don't want you to stop."

He swallowed hard, the tense line of his jaw giving evidence to his restraint. "My given name is John. I would like you to use it."

She hesitated but then nodded. She knew that inheriting the marquisate had upended his life, changing everything he believed to be true about himself. Here, when it was just the two of them, she could show him that she saw him for himself and not as the new Marquess of Lowenbrock, a title with which he was still uncomfortable.

"Yes, John."

He grasped her hand and brought it to his chest. Her fingers spread wide, taking in his heat.

He kissed her again, and everything seemed to move quickly from there. She used both hands now to explore his chest and arms, amazed at the feel of his muscles. A jolt of shyness went through her when she realized he was raising her nightdress.

The heat of his hand on her thigh almost caused her to swoon. She expected him to bring her down onto the bed and lie next to her. But instead, he lifted her and settled her on his lap, her legs on either side of his. He kept kissing her, his mouth hungry on hers, and she matched him. When he placed his hands on her hips and brought her center so it rested over the hard ridge of his arousal, she tore her mouth away and stared down at him. She was surprised to find herself panting.

He lifted his hips while bringing her body closer to his, and she couldn't hold back her slight moan. She'd never imagined this intimacy would feel so good.

"You could bring a man to the edge of reason. Promise me you'll always be mine."

She would give him anything he wanted. And if he wanted forever, why on earth would she deny him when he could elicit such wicked sensations from her? Part of her believed she was behaving selfishly, holding him to something he might not want when he realized he could have any available woman in England. But she found that she no longer cared. Lowenbrock—no, she must think of him as John now —might not love her, but it was clear he had feelings for her.

"I promise," she said, moving against his arousal.

His gaze settled on hers, and she wanted to scream with frustration when his hands on her hips stopped her motion. "You'll marry me, Amelia?"

He hadn't told her what she so wanted to hear— that he loved her—but she could see in his eyes that he cared for her. Above all, he respected her. Perhaps, together, the two were close enough to love. It was more than most had when they wed.

"Yes, I'll marry you."

His eyes searched hers for several seconds. Then, with a low growl, he flipped them until she was on her back. He hovered over her, his weight braced on his arms. "It's time to do away with the rest of our clothing."

His words shocked yet thrilled her. She wasn't wearing any undergarments under her nightdress. She stifled her initial urge to resist the suggestion, because in that moment she realized that like him, she wanted there to be nothing between them.

And so she shifted to help him remove her nightdress. She expected him to follow suit and remove the rest of his clothing, but after tossing her nightdress to the side, he dragged his eyes down her body.

Heat crept over her skin as she allowed herself to remain still under his perusal. And then he began touching her everywhere. He rested his weight on one arm and with the other began a careful exploration of her body. His hand started at her hips where they flared just below her waist and slowly crept upward. When he cupped one breast and began to toy with the nipple, a shock of sensation speared through her body.

He dipped his head, but instead of kissing her, he took the peak of her breast into his mouth.

"John." His name was a broken whisper, delight soon replacing her shock. This man knew how to please a woman and make her forget that she lay vulnerable and exposed. She wanted more.

Her hands wandered from his shoulders downward. She explored the muscles of his chest and abdomen again, tracing the ridges of muscle with curious fingers. Wondering if his nipples were as sensitive as hers, she ran her fingers over them and was rewarded with a soft groan.

His mouth drifted lower, and she began to feel a twinge of alarm when he spread her legs wide and positioned himself between them.

"What are you doing?" She barely managed the words as she tried to hold back her embarrassment.

"I'm making sure this first night is one you'll remember. Do you trust me, Amelia?"

"Since the first moment I saw you."

His gaze seemed to bore through her, and for a moment she had the irrational sensation that he was remembering their encounter in the tavern. But no, he'd forgotten about the barmaid he'd met briefly. He would think she was referring to when he first arrived at Brock Manor.

His gaze left hers, and he watched his hand as it trailed from her knee, up her inner thigh, and to her very center.

When he entered her with one finger, she was beyond caring about her embarrassment. She thought he was shifting to examine her more closely, but then he did something that had her mind going blank with shock. He kissed her there, above where his hand was stimulating her from within. She buried her fingers in his hair, thinking to pull him away, but when he licked her, the heat of his breath all but causing her to melt, she was powerless to do anything but hold him in place. She was certain of only one thing in that moment—she would die if he stopped.

It didn't take long at all before her breath quickened, her body reaching for something she'd never experienced. Then it happened. A wave of pleasure swept through her, so intense she swore she saw stars behind her eyelids. Every muscle in her body tensed as the sensation rolled through her.

John lifted his head, and Amelia opened her eyes to meet his gaze.

"I can't wait any longer," he said.

"I don't want you to."

She meant it. He'd given her pleasure she never could have imagined, but it felt hollow because she hadn't done the same for him. She wanted... No, she needed him to be right there with her.

He rose from the bed in one fluid movement, and she watched again as he finished undressing. His manhood stood straight out from his body, and she had the jarring thought that it was significantly larger than the finger he'd used to penetrate her. But she trusted that he wouldn't hurt her.

He lowered himself next to her on the bed, and this time it was her turn to explore. Every muscle in his body was tense, and she knew it cost him dearly to lie still while she ran her hands over him. She hesitated when she reached his arousal, wondering if it was unseemly for her to want to touch him there. He took the decision from her by moving her hand to him and urging her to curl her fingers around his erection.

She was surprised to find that he was both hard and soft at the same time. When she looked up, his heavy-lidded gaze was fixed on the sight of her hand on him. Some instinct had her caressing him, running her hand up and down his length. His jaw clenched, and he met her gaze.

She could see the question in his eyes. "I'm ready."

He was over her again, settling between her open legs. His mouth devoured hers, communicating his need. He shifted his hips so that his arousal rested against her entrance. She gave a hum of approval, enjoying the sensation.

She'd been wrong to think he wouldn't hurt her, because the thrust of his hips had him entering her in one swift movement that was followed by pain.

"I'm so sorry," he said, his lips moving against hers as he spoke the words. "It won't hurt next time."

He held himself still inside her, giving her body time to adjust to the intrusion, continuing to kiss her until she almost forgot the pain. His hands covered her breasts, and then he moved one to rub at the spot just above where they were joined together. The spot where he'd caused her so much pleasure with his mouth and tongue. He drew little circles with his thumb, and her body responded eagerly to the stimulation.

She was still a little tender when he drew back and entered her again, but the sharp pain was now a dull memory. After several more thrusts on his part, she found herself shifting to meet him.

He murmured words of encouragement, his hand moving to grasp one leg behind the knee and bringing it over his hip. She didn't need his guidance to do the same with her other leg before wrapping them around his waist, meeting his steady thrusts with her own.

Had she thought this painful? This was the most amazing feeling in the world.

She recognized the sensations coursing through her body now and knew she was about to reach that point of pleasure. John tore his mouth from hers and their eyes locked. She wanted to tell him that she loved him, but instead she showed him with her body.

Her breathing grew ragged, and she noticed that his sharp breaths matched hers. The wave crested then, and she called out his name while he continued to move in and out of her. Just when she thought she wouldn't be able to stand another moment, he pulled out of her and she felt a splash of hot liquid on her hip.

With a soft curse, he stood and walked over to the washbasin. He returned with two wet washcloths and used one of them to wipe up the mess he'd made. She'd learned enough to know what had just happened. He'd finished outside her body to prevent pregnancy.

When he hesitated, she rose onto her elbows. "Is something the matter?"

"There's blood. I can clean it for you if you'd like?"

Oh Lord, of course. She'd forgotten she would bleed the first time. Not all women did, or so she'd been told. But given the sharp stab of pain she'd felt when he first entered her, she wasn't surprised.

She rose to a sitting position and held out her hand in reply. When he handed her the second wash-cloth, she stood and moved behind the screen set up in one corner of her bedroom. There were some things one had to do for oneself, after all.

When she returned, he was sprawled on her bed. He'd drawn the covers up, and she slipped under them as well, snuggling against his chest. He wrapped his arms around her and held her close.

They stayed like that for several minutes, with him running a hand across her hip in small circles. She was on the verge of falling asleep when he spoke.

"Would you care to explain what you were doing working as a barmaid... Molly?"

Shock acted like a cold bucket of water poured over her. She'd known it was possible he'd recognize her once she did away with her lace caps and specta-cles, but she'd hoped he'd forgotten about that encounter. It seemed she'd underestimated the man with whom she'd just made love.

CHAPTER 24

"*A*RE YOU ANGRY?"

Her question, when it came after a long silence, was barely above a whisper. John looked down at her, but she didn't meet his gaze.

"No, of course not. But I am curious why you thought to hide this from me. Did you think I wouldn't recognize you?"

"You didn't for the longest time. And it was dark that evening."

"I thought I was imagining things when we met and you reminded me of Molly."

She winced. "When did you realize it was me?"

"When I saw you looking like sin itself in your nightdress."

She swatted him on the shoulder. "You thought I looked like sin that night?"

"I know you did, as did every other man in the tavern."

She released a soft breath. "I was uncomfortable in that dress. The woman I borrowed it from must have been tiny. I almost gave up and went home before I'd even started, but Alice—the other barmaid —convinced me to stay. Mr. Markham paid her to look out for me."

"Well, thank heavens for that. Would you care to explain why you were there to begin with?"

"I was doing research… for the book I'm writing."

He shook his head. It didn't surprise him that Amelia would think to immerse herself in that environment for the sake of her writing. Given that she no longer hid the fact she was writing a book from him and that her fingers seemed to be permanently stained with ink, it was clear she was dedicated to her craft.

Still, he had to know just how far she'd gone. "Was that night your first working as a barmaid?" He steeled himself as he waited for her reply. He hated the thought of her putting herself in such danger.

"Yes. The first and the last. I think in future I'll limit my research to interviewing people who can help me understand my characters."

He dragged her over him so her body draped over his. "I'm glad to hear that."

She bit her lower lip, and his eyes focused on the movement. "You don't mind?"

"What? That you did something dangerous for the sake of your writing?"

She nodded.

"I'm not happy about it, but at least Markham arranged to have someone watch out for you. And if I'm not mistaken, there was a man in the corner whom he'd also paid to ensure you stayed safe."

Her eyes widened in surprise. "Are you sure? He never mentioned that to me."

"The man's eyes didn't leave you all night. And when I stood to intervene, he was already out of his chair, ready to do the same. Also, I saw him outside that night after you'd left in the carriage. At first I thought his interest in you was of the unseemly sort, but now I realize he was there to ensure your safety. Given what I know about Markham, it makes sense."

Amelia shook her head. "I don't know why he didn't tell me. I wouldn't have protested."

"Perhaps he thought you would… We can ask him the next time we see him. But I have one more question to ask before I allow you to distract me again."

She raised a brow in question and waited.

"Are you close to the point where you'll allow me to read your book?"

She buried her face in his chest and he waited. He'd caught the look of horror on her face.

"If you wish to be published, you'll have to show others your writing."

She lifted her head and met his gaze. "Is it strange

that I feel more stripped bare when talking about my writing than lying in bed with you without a stitch of clothing on?"

He considered the question. "Maybe it's a combination of both happening at the same time. We could discuss this tomorrow."

Her smile widened. "And I didn't even have to distract you."

"Trust me, Amelia, the very fact you exist is a distraction. When you're pressed up against me like this, I don't stand a chance of holding on to a coherent thought."

Her smile had the power to make his heart feel lighter. He couldn't believe he hadn't realized right away this woman was the same one he'd met that night in London, but he thanked his lucky stars that she was with him now.

"You know, it occurs to me that I still have some research to do when it comes to romantic relationships. Perhaps I should put my nightdress back on and arrange to interview you?" The twinkle in her eye told him she knew very well what was about to happen after making such an outrageous statement.

He shifted them both until she was under him, his body pressing her much softer one into the mattress. He rested most of his weight on one arm so he wouldn't crush her.

"I think in this, I'll need to give you another demonstration."

Her gaze softened. "Whatever you think is best, my lord."

CHAPTER 25

July 1816

LOWENBROCK DIDN'T PRESS HER about reading her book, so she didn't have to come up with an excuse to deny him. She wasn't sure if it was because they were busy with last-minute preparations for the ball or if he realized she wasn't ready yet to share her writing.

Now that he knew they'd met before when she was serving at the tavern, she didn't have to fear being discovered. But there was still the matter of just how much she'd based the character of the hero on him, and he might not like it.

She'd started making changes in the second half of the book and was close to finishing the first draft. When that happened, she needed to go back to the beginning and change those parts of the book where the hero was almost indistinguishable from John.

She made her way to his study with the final menus for the ball. Mrs. Hastings had delivered the menus herself when Amelia had emerged from her writing session that afternoon. Amelia had already discussed with her the changes John asked her to make, but the head housekeeper wanted his formal approval. She really couldn't blame the woman for wanting to ensure everything would meet the new marquess's expectations.

It was impossible to believe the ball was only one week away. Amelia felt a mixed sense of excitement and apprehension whenever she thought about it. John's friends and family were due to arrive soon and would be staying for a few days before the event.

She was afraid they wouldn't approve of his choice of marchioness. If John changed his mind, she wouldn't force him into keeping a promise made in the heat of passion. She loved him enough to let him go. But if that came to pass, her heart would never recover.

She tapped on his closed study door and opened it when John called out for her to enter. A smile lit his face when he saw it was her.

He held his hand out to her, and she circled the desk and took it. He tugged her onto his lap, as he usually did whenever she came into this room and they were alone.

"You cannot imagine how much I needed this break. My guilt at shirking my duty this year had me asking Jeffers for assistance in becoming familiar with the workings of Parliament. I had no idea he'd set out a massive course of study on English law and parliamentary procedure."

Knowing that John liked to be prepared, she couldn't help teasing him. "You probably don't need to know all the inner workings. Just feel your way through things."

His frown spoke volumes about what he thought of her suggestion, and she couldn't hold back her laughter.

"Fine, I'll admit that I like learning. It's one of the things I regret about my youth... that I couldn't go to Oxford as I'd hoped."

John rarely spoke about his past. She'd have to dig deeper at some point, but the way he was looking at her now told her that talking was the last thing on his mind. Before he could lead them both astray, she placed the menus on his desk.

"Mrs. Hastings asked for your approval on the refreshments for the ball. She's also created menus for what we'll be serving the guests who will be staying here."

John's brows drew together. "Your approval should be enough. If you think it's fine, then I will as well. It's not as though I know anything about such things after spending the past ten years fighting on the continent."

"I did consult on the choices. But until we're wed, my opinion doesn't hold as much weight as yours."

John let out an annoyed huff. "I cannot wait to make the announcement at the ball." He turned his attention to the sheets of paper she'd placed on his desk, his eyes scanning over the lists.

While his attention wasn't fixed on her, Amelia closed her eyes for a moment and gathered her courage. When he gave a nod upon reaching the end of the pages, she took a deep breath. "We need to discuss the announcement."

His gaze settled on hers again, his eyes narrowed. "Did you change your mind about making a formal announcement in the newspapers?"

Amelia shook her head. "I know you want to introduce me as your future marchioness early in the evening, but perhaps it would be best to wait until later. If you find one of the guests better suited to the role of marchioness—"

He stopped her with a fervent but brief kiss. "That won't happen. No one could compare to you."

Amelia's heart soared at his words. She wanted desperately to believe that was true. "Perhaps we can wait until midway through the ball then?"

John released a harsh breath and leaned back in his chair. His eyes remained fixed on hers though, and she found herself wanting to squirm under the intensity of his stare. "You won't give up on this nonsense, will you?"

Amelia looked away. "It is only fair. I don't want you to feel trapped into marrying me when you haven't had a chance to see if anyone else would suit you more."

John's eyes crinkled slightly, and she wondered what he'd found so amusing. "Fine," he said, lifting one of her hands and placing a kiss in the center of its palm. "But I won't change my mind. I hope the same can be said for you?"

"No. I wouldn't continue to be with you like this if I didn't care about you."

"I'm glad to hear it. Now tell me…" He gazed down at her palm again, stroking his fingers along the ink stains that marred the skin where she held her quill. "How is your writing going?"

She tried to ignore the nonsensical, slight flare of panic at his question. She wasn't ready for him to read it.

"I've finished the first draft, but I still have much to do in edits. There are some changes I need to make. But these"—she wagged the fingers he still held in his grasp—"are from a letter I was writing. I'm not sure if I should bother sending it at this point or just hand it to her when she arrives. She'd mentioned in her last correspondence that she might be arriving earlier than planned."

"This is your friend Mary?"

Amelia nodded. "It will be nice to have her here

when your friends and family arrive. I admit I'm a little nervous about meeting them."

His head tilted to one side. "Surely you invited more of your friends?"

"Mary Trenton is my closest friend from when my parents sent me away to school. I never really became close with anyone else."

"You didn't have a governess?"

The way he stroked a thumb along her fingers and over her palm sent shivers of awareness through her. It never failed to surprise her how such a simple touch could affect her so much.

"I did, but when the staff started falling ill and one of the maids died, my parents thought it best to send me away from home. That was the last time I saw them."

He must have realized she was close to tears, because he didn't press her for further details about that time. Instead, he held on to her hand more firmly, giving her the time she needed to collect herself.

After a minute had passed, she took a deep breath and continued. "I might have picked up a bad habit of dropping into a thick Yorkshire accent to annoy my uncle when I first came to live here. After a while, I was able to leave my anger behind and he became a father figure to me."

One corner of his mouth kicked up. "That would explain your accent that night at the tavern. You have no idea how much I chastised myself when something about the way you tilted your head reminded me of that barmaid."

And here she'd thought she'd been successful in erasing all signs of their first encounter. She'd underestimated this man.

She laid her free hand along his cheek and gazed into his eyes. "If we do wed, we'll be going to London when you take your seat in the House of Lords. We'll be able to attend all manner of balls then."

"*When* we wed, I have no doubt that will happen. But I hope you don't plan on accepting every invitation."

Amelia couldn't hold back her laugh at his alarm. "Much as I would like to linger here with you, I should probably let you get back to your work. Besides, I know Mrs. Hastings is awaiting my return."

"You can tell her that I approve of the menus. And that I can't wait until the day she'll accept your word on these matters."

She leaned closer and placed a kiss on his lips. It was meant to be a quick peck but turned into a lingering one.

He stopped her when she started to stand. "Perhaps we should lock the door and forget our duties for the afternoon."

Anticipation surged at the suggestion. "We can't. Mrs. Hastings has the keys to every room in this house. She warned me to return right away or she'll hunt me down. I think she's afraid I'll disappear into my writing and forget about the menus."

He raised one brow. "Shall we test that theory? Do you really think she'll just barge in here?"

Amelia wanted nothing more than to take him up on his suggestion, but the last thing she wanted was a scandal. Despite how carefully they were behaving toward one another, there was no hiding from the servants the fact that her relationship to the marquess had changed. They were looking at her in a knowing way. And then there were the whispers that ceased when she entered a room. Of course, those whispers had always been present, but she couldn't help but think everyone was talking about the two of them now.

To avoid temptation, she pulled away and rose from his lap. "You're too conscientious to put off your work."

He crossed his arms over his chest, not bothering to hide the hint of disappointment in his voice. "And how do you know that?"

"You've thrown yourself into learning everything about the estate, working late into the night. And…" She waved a hand over the papers spread across his desk. "You won't be content to take your seat in the House of Lords without learning everything you can about what's expected of you. That speaks to a personality above reproach. We both know many wouldn't go to that trouble."

He gave his head a small shake. "You seem to have a high opinion of me."

"You know that I do. I wouldn't have agreed to your proposal if I didn't."

He was silent for several seconds. "Would you care to share your northern accent with me?"

She couldn't hold back her embarrassment at his request. "You've already heard it once."

"I'm curious. I can't help but wonder if you'll suddenly morph into the barmaid before my eyes."

There was a hint of something in his eyes that she didn't understand. "I've already admitted that I am."

"Yes, but it might be fun. You can pretend to be the barmaid again, and I'll pretend to be a customer who wants a different type of service."

Her mouth dropped open in shock. Good heavens, did people actually engage in such role-play? The thought scandalized her, but if she was being completely honest, it also sent a wave of heat through her. Perhaps it wouldn't be so bad to pretend.

She leaned close and spoke in her native accent. She might have made it a little thicker on purpose to see how he would react. "Perhaps another time."

One corner of his mouth kicked up, but before he could reach for her again, she snatched the menus from the desk and danced away from his reach.

His laughter followed her out the door. She had no doubt he'd make good on their little game later, and heaven help her, she was looking forward to it.

CHAPTER 26

*O*NLY THREE MONTHS had passed since John left London for his new life. At the time, he'd been certain he would never feel at home at Brock Manor. While he still had to resist the urge to cringe whenever someone called him by his title, he'd settled into his role with relative ease.

It helped that he had an exemplary staff. Jeffers, in particular, was very patient. John's most difficult lesson had been learning how to let go. He didn't need to keep every scrap of information in his head as long as he had access to it when required.

His relationship with Amelia had helped him adjust to this new life. While he'd respected her as a friend and enjoyed her company a great deal, their romantic relationship meant everything to him.

Now, as he awaited Ashford and Cranston's

arrival, it felt like a year had passed since he'd last seen his friends.

The sun was beginning to set when their carriage drew to a halt outside the manse. John had left word he was to be summoned as soon as they arrived and so he was waiting outside when his friends stepped down from the carriage.

"Deuced take it, that was a long ride," Ashford said when he caught sight of John. "I don't think I've ever been this far north. Are you sure we aren't in Scotland?"

Cranston stepped forward and grasped John's hand in greeting. "I thought Ashford would stop complaining when we arrived. It appears I underestimated the man."

John laughed, happiness filling his soul as he turned to shake the hand Ashford extended. "Welcome to Brock Manor."

Cranston whistled low as his eyes swept over the house. "When you decide to fall into a surprise inheritance, you don't do things by half measures."

He'd been the untitled member of their group, and he was a little uncomfortable at the notion that he now outranked his two friends. "I still can't believe it myself. I wake up far too often thinking I'm still in France and that this new life is a dream."

Ashford sobered at the reminder. "I've had those same dreams." He shook his head as if to clear the memories from his mind. "We were surprised to get your letter. Thought you'd last a little longer than three months before begging us to visit. But you didn't need to throw a ball as inducement."

John led the way into the house, his friends flanking him. "No one is more annoyed by this than me. But it was either host a ball and meet the neighbors in one go or suffer through an unending parade of callers all curious to meet me."

Cranston winced in sympathy. "Wait until they see you. A young marquess, not too ugly. The mamas will be swarming you all night."

"I think you meant to say they'll be swarming *us* all evening." A corner of John's mouth lifted as the two men frowned in unison. If he had to suffer through the unwanted scrutiny, at least he wouldn't be alone.

Ashford narrowed his eyes. "Cranston and I managed to avoid all the matchmaking this past season. I never thought you'd betray us in this way."

"We'll get through it, chaps," Cranston said, clapping John on the shoulder. "Even if it threatens to kill us. But just remember, you owe us a favor for inducing suffering above and beyond the call of duty."

"We suffered through countless battles," John said. "How difficult can this be?"

"Famous last words, my friend." Cranston gave his head a small shake. "I was dragged to a few balls before I enlisted. To say they can be tedious is an understatement."

"Well, at least I'll be getting the ordeal of meeting the neighbors over with in one evening. A ball is preferable to sitting through countless visits and having to turn down all those dinner invitations."

Ashford let out a bark of laughter. "You're mistaken if you think a ball will get you out of the invitations. Especially if they decide one of their daughters should be your marchioness. It's quiet now because they've been in London. Soon enough, the invitations will commence again."

John let out a soft curse. "Well, thanks for the warning. Clearly I have no idea what I'm in for when it comes to society. At any rate, dinner will be served within the hour. I'll have someone show you to your rooms and see you then. Oh, and please be on your best behavior. There is a lady in residence."

Just as he knew it would, that revelation had both men raising their brows. John was saved from their questions about the woman's identity when a footman arrived to escort them to their rooms. But if either of them remembered Amelia as the barmaid he'd assisted in the tavern, there would be no escaping their curiosity.

He could only shake his head in amusement as the young footman led them from the room with instructions that their valets would be available shortly. A glance out the drawing room window showed him that a second carriage was arriving. He stood and watched as arrangements were made to have trunks brought around to the servants' entrance. The two older gentlemen, no doubt the valets in question, stood back and allowed Hastings to orchestrate the arrangements.

"Is there anything I can do while we wait for dinner to be served?"

He turned at the sound of Amelia's voice. She wore a rose-colored dress that brought out the color in her cheeks and underscored her beauty. Fortunately, it had a modest décolletage. The last thing he needed was for his friends to become overly friendly with the woman he intended to wed.

He wasn't aware he was frowning until he saw Amelia's smile vanish. "Did you want me to take dinner in my room tonight?"

He reached for her hands, holding them lightly within his, and shook his head. "Of course not. I was just thinking that with how beautiful you look I'll have a difficult time trying to keep my friends from attempting to monopolize your attention."

She smiled. "I'm sure I'll be able to resist their charms."

"You'd better," he said, somehow managing to smooth out his frown.

The sound of a throat being cleared had him dropping her hands and stepping back. He looked up to find Hastings standing in the hallway, his expression impassive. Well, it wasn't as though the entire staff wasn't already gossiping about them.

"Yes?"

"Your guests have been shown to their rooms, and their valets are on their way to attend them. Was there anything else you required before dinner is served?"

John looked down at his own attire and released a frustrated breath. There would be no doing things by half measures now that they had guests staying with them. "I was just heading upstairs myself. You can ask Oliver to attend me. The man will be thrilled to finally have the opportunity to 'dress me properly.'"

He exited the room to the sound of Amelia's amused laughter.

CHAPTER 27

*T*IME TO HERSELF AS SHE WAITED for dinner did nothing to ease Amelia's nerves. She and John had agreed that they wouldn't reveal their relationship until midway through the ball, but that didn't calm her in the least. She wanted his friends to like her, but she wasn't nearly as witty in person as she was on the page. She feared they would find her lacking in all manner of ways. For that reason, she'd taken great care when dressing to look her best.

She needed a distraction, and what better way to take her mind from the upcoming dinner than to immerse herself in someone else's world. With that goal in mind, she made her way down the hall to the library.

Her uncle hadn't been a fan of fiction, but over the years she'd used a portion of her funds to buy some of the more popular titles. She wandered over to the shelf he'd set aside for her books and let out a sigh. She'd already read through her meager collection. She'd hoped to visit one of the circulating libraries when she was in London to learn what members of the ton were clamoring for, but her visit had been cut short before she'd been able to do so.

She settled for a reread of *The Castle of Otranto*. It was a slim volume and had started the trend of what many called "horrid" novels. She preferred the term *Gothic* herself, hating the judgment inherent in the more popularly used term. Her gaze fell on *The Mysteries of Udolpho*, and she took that book to set aside for later. She'd have to wait until she had more time to read the much longer book by Mrs. Radcliffe.

She was halfway through Horace Walpole's story when she was drawn out of the fictional world of a haunted castle and family curses by the sound of loud male voices. John and his friends were coming down the stairs together.

With a deep breath, she put the book aside. The story had served to take her mind from the upcoming meeting, but her nerves came rushing back as she made her way to the drawing room.

She hesitated on the threshold, examining the men who hadn't yet noticed her arrival. They were laughing at something one of them had said, and it warmed her heart to see the man she loved enjoying the company of his friends. She was probably biased in thinking he was the most handsome man in the room, but the way his fair hair shone in the candle-light never failed to capture her attention.

The other men were dark-haired and also attractive. John had told her they were unattached, and she could well imagine the stir the three men would cause at the ball.

As if sensing her perusal, John glanced her way. He raised one brow and waited for her to gather the courage to join them. He must have sensed her trepidation, because he didn't draw their attention to her.

After taking a deep breath, she squared her shoulders and stepped into the room.

John's friends turned her way, and she found herself the subject of their scrutiny. She wanted to examine their expressions to see if they recognized her from that night at the tavern but knew it would seem too forward. Instead, she waited as John made his way to her side.

"Miss Amelia Weston," he said with a bow. "Allow me to introduce these two ruffians to you. My good friends Viscount Ashford and Baron Cranston. Gentlemen, I present to you Miss Amelia Weston, niece to the late Marquess of Lowenbrock."

They inclined their heads, and she curtsied, doing her best to ignore her nerves. Not since that evening at the tavern had she been the subject of such intense male scrutiny. Unlike that time, however, she didn't feel that these men had any ill intentions toward her.

They were definitely curious, but they gave no indication of recognizing her.

Ashford smiled. "It is a pleasure to meet you, Miss Weston. Lowenbrock didn't tell us that the marquess had such a lovely niece or that we'd have the pleasure of meeting you today."

John had warned her that his friends would be flirtatious but that their attention would be harmless. They'd never force themselves on someone who didn't welcome it.

"Well, he has told me quite a bit about you and Lord Cranston."

Cranston chuckled. "We're in trouble now, Ashford."

The viscount raised a shoulder. "I welcome the opportunity to get to know you."

Cranston's brow furled. "It's the oddest thing. I feel as though we've met before."

Amelia's stomach dipped. She and John had discussed this eventuality. It was clear the baron couldn't place her. She hadn't served them that evening, so his friends had only seen her from afar. They would never realize she was the barmaid John had helped.

Her gaze never wavered as she smiled. "I am certain we've never been introduced."

"Of course not," Cranston said with a small shake of his head. "You remind me of someone, but for the life of me I can't say who."

Amelia was saved from replying when the butler arrived to tell them that dinner would soon be served. She took John's arm and allowed him to lead her and his friends to the dining room. Now that she didn't have to worry about one of these men recognizing her, her sense of relief was profound.

CHAPTER 28

THEY FELL INTO AN EASY PATTERN over the next few days. Amelia was so busy she barely had time to look at her manuscript, let alone get started on the edits to her book. But she did find time to go through the first half of the book, before the hero had changed, and list all the instances where she'd borrowed too heavily from John's behavior.

She mulled over the opening for some time but couldn't bring herself to consider changing the tavern scene. She needed to talk to him about her book. She was behaving like a coward and couldn't put off the discussion much longer.

It would have to wait a little while longer, however. Since his friends' arrival, John was circumspect in his behavior toward her, even avoiding her bedroom at night. She understood his caution but missed him nonetheless.

John took his friends riding on the day of Mary's arrival. If it weren't so early in the afternoon, she'd have thought they were heading into town to visit the local tavern. For all she knew, they were doing that anyway.

She was in the ballroom, helping to direct the footmen in setting up the refreshment table and the seating areas, when the butler entered.

"A carriage is approaching, Miss Weston."

She beamed at the man. "Thank you so much, Hastings." She turned to the housekeeper. "I can return later if you need me…"

Mrs. Hastings gave her head a little shake. "We have things well in hand here. Go enjoy the rest of the day with your guest."

Amelia thanked her and hurried down the hall and out onto the front steps. It had been so long since she'd seen Mary—nine years. They'd maintained their friendship through correspondence, but it wasn't the same as spending time together.

She watched the footman open the carriage door and help her friend step down. When Mary's gaze locked on Amelia, her smile widened.

Amelia rushed to cover the short distance between them and embraced her friend before stepping back to examine her. "I cannot tell you how happy I am to see you! Thank you for accepting our invitation."

Mary's gaze wandered over her. "The years have

been good to you. You're even more beautiful than I remember."

"Oh hush," Amelia said, linking her arm through Mary's and leading her into the house.

Her friend had always insisted that Amelia was the pretty one of the two, but she far underestimated her own appeal. Mary had a liveliness of spirit that did much to elevate what she considered her ordinary appearance. Tendrils of light brown hair framed her face, which was slimmer now than Amelia remembered. Her features had always seemed too big for her face—wide eyes, a wide mouth, and a nose that was just a touch too broad at the base. But no one would ever accuse Mary Trenton of being ordinary.

Amelia had instructed the staff to prepare refreshments as soon as the carriage arrived. The two had just settled onto the settee when a footman arrived with a tray of tea and biscuits.

Amelia placed a slice of cake on a plate for her friend and poured two cups of tea.

"You are an angel," Mary said, taking a sip of the tea first before reaching for the plate. Her eyes roved over the assortment of biscuits and cakes on the tray. "You're going to spoil me with all my favorites."

"I have to make the trip worth your while so you'll be willing to do it again in future."

"The treats are an added bonus but not necessary. Simply providing me with the opportunity to escape my sister's household is inducement enough."

Amelia took a sip of her own tea. "I'm sorry to hear things are still so tense between you."

"It's as though she blames me for our parents' deaths and the house falling to the next male heir. She had her choice of suitors. I certainly didn't advise her to wed the wealthiest—and oldest—from among them. That was her choice."

"You never let on that she was unhappy."

Mary lifted a shoulder in a casual shrug. "She reads my correspondence, so I can't be completely honest in my letters."

"What?" Mary's admission shocked Amelia. But it did account for all the times Mary hadn't offered information about what was going on in her life. "Why would she do that?"

"Your guess is as good as mine. Maybe she thinks I'm in danger of starting a torrid love affair via correspondence. I think she's determined I should stay a spinster."

"You're of age. She wouldn't be able to stop you from marrying whomever you choose."

"Yes, but she can make the courtship difficult. Not that anyone would ask to court me, an old maid of five and twenty."

Amelia placed a hand on her friend's arm. She hadn't wanted to blurt out the truth about her relationship with John, but she could no longer hold back. If she didn't tell *someone*, she felt as though she would burst. It had been difficult pretending they were nothing more than acquaintances when his friends were in the room with them.

"I might be in a position to aid you soon."

Mary placed her cup of tea on the table and took hold of Amelia's hand. "I sincerely hope you're not about to play matchmaker between me and the new marquess. I'm happy enough unwed. Given the way my sister looks at her husband at times, I'm not eager to find myself in a similar unhappy situation. Witnessing their marriage is more than enough for me."

"No, of course not." Amelia's lips twisted at the suggestion, and her friend let out a peal of laughter. She lowered her voice and leaned in closer. "Lord Lowenbrock has asked me to marry him, and I have accepted."

Mary seemed to freeze in place, and this time it was Amelia's turn to laugh.

"It's true. We have an agreement. As long as he doesn't find someone else who captures his interest at the ball, we'll be making an announcement."

Mary crossed her arms. "So this is a typical society marriage. Tell me you at least like him."

"I love him. And he is so handsome." She didn't bother to try to hide the yearning she felt whenever she thought of John, and her friend's mouth turned up in a genuine smile.

"I'm so happy to hear that. If anyone deserves to be happy, it is you."

"We *both* deserve it. And once Lowenbrock and I are wed, I can help you find a husband as well."

Mary let out a sigh and reached for one of the small cakes. "Tell me all about this marquess of yours."

Amelia had opened her mouth to do just that when they were interrupted by the sound of the front door opening, followed by the jumble of male voices and laughter. John and his friends had returned.

"You'll see him for yourself soon enough," Amelia said, folding her hands in her lap and trying to hold back the grin that threatened to reveal her emotions to John's friends.

Seconds later, the men entered the drawing room. She and Mary stood, and Amelia made the introductions.

Ashford's smile widened as he tilted his head to examine Mary, who'd dipped into a curtsy.

"I believe I already have the pleasure of knowing Miss Trenton. Your family hails from Norfolk if I'm correct."

"You are. If I recall, you broke my sister's heart when you enlisted."

Ashford raised a brow. "I can assure you there was nothing between the two of us. I barely remember her."

"Oh, I know, and that vexed her greatly. She's now wed and is Lady Fairbanks."

He gave a wry laugh. "And your parents are in good health?"

"Sadly, my parents passed away. My sister has been kind enough to allow me to live with her."

"I'm sorry to hear that. My condolences on your loss."

Mary inclined her head in acknowledgment.

"Well, I'm sure you gentlemen are famished," Amelia said. "Lord Lowenbrock always likes to have a little something to eat when he returns from one of his rides."

John smiled at her, and she had to look away lest she betray herself.

"I'll show my friend to her room. We've barely begun to catch up. I'm sure the three of you know something about that."

"Of course," Lord Cranston said with a slight bow. "It is a pleasure making your acquaintance, Miss Trenton. I look forward to getting to know you better."

Amelia watched the man carefully for a moment, her thoughts beginning to whirl as she imagined how perfect it would be if Mary were to form an attachment to one of John's friends.

There would be time for such speculation later. For now, she threaded her hand through Mary's arm and led her from the room. She wouldn't push the two of them together, but it wouldn't hurt to keep an eye on the situation.

CHAPTER 29

*J*OHN WOKE THAT MORNING with a sense of anticipation. Today his sisters would arrive.

He'd been disappointed to learn they weren't bringing his nieces and nephews, but he understood their reasons. It didn't make sense to subject them to such a long carriage ride for a short visit. Maybe next summer, after he and Amelia were wed, they'd be in a position to invite his family for a much longer stay.

He smiled as he imagined the scene while his valet set out the clothing he would be wearing that day. Perhaps Amelia would be round with child then. They'd taken care to ensure she wouldn't fall pregnant before marrying, but one could never be completely certain it wouldn't happen anyway. The sooner he married her, the better.

He'd left London on good terms with his sisters and their husbands, but a part of him had wanted to escape their constant hovering. Now, only three months later, he couldn't wait to see them again.

He'd fallen into the pattern of his new life with surprising ease. So much so that hosting his two friends at Brock Manor set him off-balance at first. And today he would be welcoming his sisters and their spouses. Another landmark in that life.

His friends were already awake when he reached the main floor, having fallen in with his daily habit of going for a ride first thing in the morning.

Together, they ventured farther than he normally did when he was alone, but with the ball only two days away, he knew Amelia wouldn't be waiting to have breakfast with him. Since his friends' arrival, she'd taken to having breakfast sent to her room. Afterward, she spent the rest of the morning occupied with whatever it was women did when a social event they were about to host was fast approaching.

His friends took every opportunity to remark on his good fortune at being so far from his family. Their own relations—who'd been happy to send them off to war—now seemed intent on seeing them settled and producing children.

It felt decadent to spend days with his friends. Riding, taking their meals together, engaging in a rousing game of billiards. The days were worlds apart from how they'd spent the past few years together.

Jeffers was handling the day-to-day running of the estate, but John couldn't quell the itch under his skin that seemed to prod him to do more. He'd never been a man of leisure, and it seemed he was now too old to start.

It didn't help that he rarely caught a glimpse of Amelia throughout the day. Seeing her only when they all gathered for dinner wasn't enough for him.

It was fast approaching the dinner hour when a footman interrupted their billiard game to inform him that his family's carriages were approaching. He'd played so often over the past two days that he'd gone from being the worst player to coming close to Ashford's considerable skill.

Ashford put away his cue and began to retrieve the billiard balls, setting them up for their next game. "Saved from the ignominy of defeat at the hands of a novice."

Cranston chuckled. "He's fast outstripped my meager skill. I can't wait to see the look on your face when he defeats you."

"Perhaps, but that day has yet to arrive."

John clapped them on the back and took his leave without another word. He'd always been amused by the rivalry that existed between his two friends, but in that moment he wanted only to see his family again.

His friends caught up and flanked him as he made his way to the front hall.

"You never did tell us who your sisters married."

It was a question Cranston had asked several times, but John had always sidestepped the issue. Until his return to England, it was because he felt lacking in comparison. But that was no longer true.

"My eldest sister is married to the Marquess of Overlea and the other to the Earl of Kerrick."

Ashford whistled. "That's pretty lofty company, but then again I can now count a marquess as one of my good friends."

John grunted a noncommittal response, then nodded to the butler as he passed before striding outside. Two carriages had just drawn to a halt several feet away. His friends stood back and watched the scene unfold in silence.

John watched, anticipation curling within, as his brothers-in-law stepped down from their separate carriages and turned to help their wives. Catherine emerged first and turned toward him. The smile that spread across her face seemed to reach right inside him and squeeze his heart.

When he turned to look for his eldest sister, he saw the way she smiled at her husband as he helped her down. Overlea gazed down at his wife with a fondness that caused a small pang of remorse to go through him. They'd already made amends, yet he wasn't sure he'd ever be able to forgive himself for the way he'd treated this man in the past.

He met his sisters halfway as they threw themselves into his arms.

Catherine stepped back first, but Louisa gripped him for several seconds longer before doing the same.

"It is so good to see you again," his elder sister said.

He gave a small huff of amusement at her tendency toward exaggeration. "It's only been three months."

"That may be, but I have ten years of missing you to make up for."

Overlea clapped him on the shoulder and drew his wife back. "It is good to see you again, Lowenbrock."

John made a face. "I'm not sure I'll ever get used to that."

His brother-in-law gave him a look that said he well understood the sentiment. With an older brother who'd passed away unexpectedly, Overlea had never expected to inherit the title.

Kerrick moved to his wife's side and greeted him with warmth.

Catherine slid her arm through his. "I thought my husband was having fun at my expense when he told me you were hosting a ball."

"Believe me, it wasn't at the top of my list of things I needed to do."

Louisa, who'd taken her husband's arm as well, tilted her head to one side. "Then why hold it? I doubt anyone would have counted it against you if you'd waited until next year."

"It was either hold a ball and meet everyone in the neighboring areas at once or suffer through an unending parade of calls from lords who wanted me to meet their unwed daughters."

Kerrick shot Overlea a knowing look. "Welcome to our world. The only solution is to wed."

Catherine frowned at her husband. "And even then, there is no end to the women who want to have a liaison with your husband."

"We can't be held responsible for what others attempt," Overlea said with a small chuckle. But the frown Louisa aimed his way had him turning it into a cough.

"Yes, well, at least I won't be the sole recipient of the neighbors' machinations."

He turned to Ashford and Cranston and made the introductions, and then the groups returned to the house.

"How are the children doing? I'm sure they'll miss you while you're away."

"I'm sure they will." Louisa's smile was bright, but John knew from the way her eyebrows drew together for a brief moment that she missed them as well. "They're staying with His Grace and their brood."

"His Grace?" Ashford aimed a curious glance at John.

"The Duke of Clarington," Overlea said. "The children are the best of friends, and we take turns hosting them at our houses for a month over the summer. It worked out that this year it was their turn."

Catherine gave him a sly glance. "Perhaps after this ball, you'll also be well on your way to starting your own families." She smiled at his friends.

As one, the two men coughed, and John couldn't hold back his bark of laughter. They cast a strange look his way, and he realized he might have tipped his hand about his future plans.

"Someone will see you to your rooms. But first I'd like a chance to speak to my sisters alone."

"Of course," Cranston said. "This will give Ashford the opportunity to brush up on his billiard skills."

Ashford glared at him, and John knew that if his sisters weren't present, he would have fouled the air with a ripe curse.

"Billiards?" Kerrick raised a brow. "I might join you in a bit. It wouldn't hurt to brush up on my skills as well."

Overlea gave his head a shake. "Don't allow this shark fleece you into betting any money."

A corner of Kerrick's mouth kicked up. "You can't blame a man for trying."

The men left and headed their separate ways—Overlea and Kerrick following the footmen upstairs and his friends heading back to the billiard room.

John inclined his head toward the drawing room and then followed his sisters there.

"I don't think I've ever been this far north before." Louisa made her way to the settee and sat, Catherine following suit.

"Indeed," Catherine said with a wry tilt of her head. "Are we still in England?"

John dropped onto an armchair with a groan. Ashford had made the same joke. "You could have stayed home if you didn't want to make the trip."

Louisa shook her head. "We're just teasing. Now tell us how things are going. Truly. It looks like you've settled in nicely but we'd be more than happy to lend our assistance."

Some things in life remained ever constant. Louisa's desire to jump in and take everyone's burdens onto her own shoulders was one of them. That tendency had bothered him in the past, making him believe that she saw him as little more than a child. But now he realized it came from a place of love and wanting only to help ease his burdens.

"Everything here is fine. But there is one thing I want to tell you."

Catherine leaned forward. "Don't be coy with us."

He chuckled. While Louisa's first tendency was to assume something horrible had happened, Catherine's was to display an unending amount of curiosity.

"I've already explained the reason for hosting the ball—"

"You've already met someone!" Catherine almost bounced in her seat as she straightened.

His sisters shared a meaningful glance before Louisa spoke.

"Is that true? We'll be meeting someone at the ball who has already caught your attention?"

"Not exactly." He almost laughed at the twin expressions of disappointment on his sisters' faces. "The former marquess has a niece who is still in residence. We've formed an attachment, and she has accepted my proposal of marriage."

This time Catherine did bounce as she reached for Louisa's hand and extended her other hand toward John. He leaned forward to grasp it, unable to restrain his grin.

"That is wonderful," Catherine said, squeezing his hand. "I'm so happy for you."

Louisa reached out to add a hand to theirs. "This is joyous news indeed. When will we be able to meet her?"

John placed his other hand over those of his sisters, giving them one last squeeze before releasing them and leaning back. "She'll be joining us for dinner. And while I don't expect you to keep this from your husbands, I would ask that you not discuss it with anyone else before the announcement is made."

A small frown formed between Catherine's brows. "You haven't told your friends?"

Louisa laughed. "He means to use them as a

shield against the unattached women when he breaks their hearts."

John winced. That wasn't precisely true, but he couldn't deny his friends wouldn't be happy to learn they'd be the only bachelors at the ball.

"Actually, I thought to spare Miss Weston the embarrassment of speculation. But I realize now that tongues will wag regardless."

"So you are planning to tell them?" One corner of Louisa's mouth rose as though she already knew his response.

"Well, now that you've raised the very practical issue of having a shield in place…"

His sisters burst into laughter.

"You are terrible," Catherine said. "They're going to murder you for not giving them any warning."

"I have no doubt they'll exact some form of revenge, but that is a problem for another time. First we have to survive the ball."

"And you said we'll meet her today?" Louisa asked as she rose to her feet.

Catherine followed suit, as did he.

"Of course. She's nervous, and I think the added guests will help. Her friend, Miss Mary Trenton, is also visiting."

"That's silly. I'm sure we'll like her just fine." Louisa's brow furled in concentration. "As for Miss Trenton, I don't think I've met her."

"I believe I have. She's the sister to Baron Fairbanks's wife. It was only the one time, however. If she joins them in town when Parliament is in session, she doesn't make it a habit of frequenting the social events."

Louisa had fallen quiet, but the stiff set of her shoulders telegraphed her concern. John knew exactly what she was thinking. He didn't particularly want to have this conversation, but it would be best to get it out of the way.

"You're worried."

He could tell that Louisa was trying to hide her doubts, but even after all these years, he could still tell when she was preparing herself to deliver bad news. The way she clenched her hands together hadn't changed. Nor the way she squared her shoulders before meeting his gaze.

"When you left England and joined the army all those years ago, you were angry because I had agreed to wed Nicholas."

"Can you blame me? All I knew about the man was that he was the head of the family that had destroyed ours. I was young and impetuous back then, and I judged him before getting to know him. But I'm glad everything worked out between the two of you, and between Catherine and Kerrick."

"I have to ask…" Louisa took a deep breath before continuing. "You gave up the future my marriage would have provided you, insisting you could find some form of employment to help the family. Are you sure you're not doing the same thing here? Sacrificing your future to save Miss Weston?"

He'd already given that matter some thought. Especially since he knew his friends would tease him again about rushing in to rescue unprotected women. But he'd long since come to the realization that his feelings for Amelia went far beyond duty.

"I understand why you feel the need to ask. And setting aside the fact that you did exactly what you're accusing me of when you wed Overlea, I want to assure you that isn't the case here. The way I feel about Amelia…" He had to look away for a moment to regain his composure. "There is no comparison between the two situations. I do want to take care of her, but I feel so much more for her."

Catherine sighed. "You love her."

John paused for a moment to consider her words. Love in a marriage wasn't something that was expected among the ton. It was true he hadn't been raised as the heir to the Lowenbrock title, but that didn't mean he'd expected to find someone he could claim to love in a romantic fashion. After all, Louisa had married for practical reasons. It wasn't until he saw her with her husband now, and Catherine with Kerrick, that he'd realized they both had relationships built on love.

And the way he felt about Amelia… She lit up a room with her mere presence. Her wit, her beauty, her intelligence… He was also proud of her desire to

238

become an author. He couldn't imagine living his life without her. She brought joy and a sense of belonging into his life that he couldn't imagine being without.

He smiled. "Yes, I do."

Louisa tilted her head and examined him for a moment. "But you haven't told her."

"Excuse me?" He crossed his arms, not caring if the action might appear defensive.

"Have you told her that you love her?" Catherine asked.

He felt his chest tighten. She did know he loved her, didn't she? "Miss Weston knows that I care for her—I've told her as much. And I did propose marriage."

Louisa took one of his arms and Catherine the other, both wearing expressions of indulgent exasperation.

"You need to give her the words," Louisa said. "I know men like to believe their actions should be proof of just how much they care, but women like to hear those three words."

"Those words being 'I love you,'" Catherine added.

John glared at her. "Thank you for explaining."

Catherine shrugged and reached up to place a kiss on his cheek. "I'm only trying to help."

Louisa did the same on his other cheek and stepped away. "Now, can you have someone show us where you've hidden our husbands?"

John shook his head in exasperation and rang for a footman to do just that. Much as he didn't want to admit it even to himself, he realized his sisters might just know a thing or two about a woman's feelings. He hated when they were right.

CHAPTER 30

JOHN'S PALMS WERE SWEATY and his emotions on edge as he waited the allocated half an hour before leaving his bedchamber. Oliver had been in raptures as he draped each garment on John's body. He'd chosen a cornflower-blue coat, pairing it with a gold-colored waistcoat. John felt like a peacock, but he trusted the man wouldn't make him look ridiculous.

His valet was of middle age and average height, but the excitement of the evening took years off the man. Oliver started to hum as he took his time tying an elaborate knot in John's cravat. The tune rubbed up against his nerves, but the man was so happy John didn't have the heart to tell him to stop.

And now he was left to pace while people entered his house. His bedroom was set toward the back of the house, so he couldn't hear the front door, but it was two floors above the ballroom. As the minutes crept by, he became aware of the soft hum of voices increasing in volume.

The soft knock at the door, when it finally came, had him rushing to answer it. Surely facing the crowd downstairs couldn't be worse than the interminable waiting.

He expected to find a footman on the other side of the door. Instead, he saw a much-changed Amelia.

He hadn't thought she could be more beautiful than she appeared when they made love, her dark hair spread in waves across his pillow, the heat of her desire tingeing her cheeks a light pink while the deep blue of her eyes deepened even further.

The vision standing before him now wasn't the passionate woman he held in his arms at night—one whom he'd missed sorely since his friends and family had descended on Brock Manor. No, this woman was dressed formally, no hint of the heat she exhibited with him in sight, but she threatened to take his breath away.

Her dark hair was up, a riot of loose curls left to frame her pale face. The medium blue gown she wore matched his coat, and he wondered if that had been a coincidence on the part of his valet.

His gaze was drawn to her bosom, which was almost on full display. It wouldn't be considered scandalous, but the amount of flesh shown was distracting. He was contemplating pulling her into the room to test just how much farther he could drag down the fabric of her décolletage. Perhaps if he was careful, all the way down.

The sound of a throat clearing had him raising his gaze away from the tempting sight. One that he realized would be a spectacle for every other man present. It didn't matter that most of the women present would likely be dressed in a similar fashion.

"Do I pass inspection?"

The glint of amusement in her eyes told him that she knew exactly what he'd been thinking.

"You certainly do. Perhaps we can hide out in here for the rest of the evening."

"And risk having your sisters come searching for you?" She gave an exaggerated shudder and placed a hand on his arm to drag him out of his chambers.

"I thought you were getting along well with Louisa and Catherine? They certainly seem to approve of you."

She'd threaded her arm through his but stopped to look up at him. "Did you tell them about us?"

"That you've agreed to marry me? Of course."

She let out a soft sigh. "That would explain why they've been so effusive in their welcome."

"That's a good thing, Amelia."

He knew exactly what she was going to say before she spoke. "You could meet someone tonight—"

He dragged her into his arms and kissed her soundly, ending her nonsense. "Never."

She looked at him with such fond exasperation.

"We should get this over with," he said, leading her toward the stairs.

"Such a dour expression for such a handsome man. The young women will be dazzled tonight."

He ignored her baiting, concentrating only on her compliment as they made their way downstairs.

It bothered him that she was still fixated on their guests and the possibility that he might cast her aside for someone else. Clearly his sisters were correct and he needed to tell her that he loved her. He considered telling her now but discarded that thought. Blurting out the truth when they were about to be accosted by the crowd gathered in the ballroom wasn't the best time. No, he needed to tell her when they were alone.

As they neared the bottom of the stairs, he became aware of the servants' gazes on them. He nodded in their direction and led Amelia down the hallway toward the back of the house. The murmur of voices from the ballroom grew louder with every step.

Seeking to lighten the tense mood that had developed between them, he leaned down and spoke in a loud whisper. "I'm having grave reservations about this."

She laughed and met his gaze, and he was pleased to see that some of her tension had eased.

"It's too late for regrets, my lord."

He let out an exaggerated breath. "How many people did you invite?"

Her smile widened. "Everyone."

Her reply caused a momentary jolt of alarm, which only served to increase her amusement.

They'd reached the ballroom doors, and so he released her arm. By the end of the night, they wouldn't have to hide their relationship. That fact alone had him straightening his spine and preparing for the task at hand. Meeting "everyone."

Amelia entered the ballroom before him, alone, and the voices in the room grew quiet. He wondered if that was for her or because they realized he would be announced after her. He was about to step forward when a footman raised a hand to signal that he wait.

"Miss Amelia Lily Weston, niece to the former Marquess of Lowenbrock."

The unmistakable sound of his butler's deep, formal tones had John wanting to curse. No one had told him they'd planned to announce their entrances. Until that moment, he'd hoped to slide into the room and find allies among his friends and family before being accosted by his guests. Those hopes were now dashed.

The footman who'd asked him to wait tilted his head in encouragement, and John knew that was his signal to proceed. He took a deep breath, admonishing himself silently for feeling as though he were stepping into battle when this event would be nothing like the real thing, and walked into the ballroom.

Which now seemed much smaller than the large, airy room he'd seen on his formal tour of the house. Bodies filled every inch of space, and he had the distracted thought that perhaps they'd invited so many people there would be no room for dancing.

"The Marquess of Lowenbrock, hero at the Battle of Waterloo."

John managed to keep the frown from his face. He was no hero, no more than any other soldier who'd fought during that battle. And certainly no more than the many who had fallen during the long, bloody war against Napoleon.

Every eye in the room was trained on him and he realized that he had no idea what he was supposed to do. And then everyone spoke again, heads bowed to their neighbors as they discussed him.

Damn, this was almost worse than entering battle.

Movement to his right had him bracing for heaven only knew what—someone wanting to throw their unwed daughter into his arms, no doubt. His tension eased when he saw his brothers-in-law move to flank him. Next to them stood his two friends.

The Marquess of Overlea leaned closer. "They're going to line up now to meet you, and then you can lead the first dance. We'll stay for moral support. I know this part can be overwhelming."

John nodded his thanks, the small gesture doing

nothing to show his immense gratitude to this man whom he'd once hated on sight. But Overlea had changed his sisters' lives for the better, and now, it seemed, he was willing to extend that support to him.

Surrounded by family and friends, he turned to face the line of guests that was forming to meet him.

CHAPTER 31

ESET BY DOUBT, Amelia watched the unending parade of guests going out of their way to curry favor with the new marquess. She'd expected as much, but it still bothered her. Every time he was introduced to another young woman, she held her breath.

He approached her after going through all the introductions, bowing low and looking more handsome than she'd ever seen him. A frisson of awareness had gone through her when he requested she join him in opening the first set. Which was silly considering everything they'd already done together.

His bow when he deposited her next to Mary had been formal, but there had been a glint in his eyes when his gaze met hers that told her she didn't need to be concerned about rivals.

She tried not to spend every moment watching

him, but she couldn't help but be aware of his presence. It was painfully evident that every eligible woman in the room—of which there were many—had set their cap for the man she loved. He hadn't shown any interest in them beyond polite courtesy, but that didn't stop them from vying for his attention. She had to turn away far too often to prevent her jealousy from becoming obvious to everyone.

She'd already danced with the Marquess of Overlea and the Earl of Kerrick, and John's friends had taken their turns dancing with her. Still, she was acutely conscious of the speculative glances thrown her way. An unwed woman living unchaperoned with the very handsome marquess… Of course there were whispers. She pretended not to hear them as she made her way back to her friend's side after taking a moment to speak to the staff to ensure the evening was going smoothly. She imagined John's sisters were dancing, yet again, with their husbands.

She linked arms with Mary and led them toward the refreshment table.

Mary leaned closer and spoke in a whisper. "I can't believe how forward some of these women are being. Would you like me to accidentally spill a few drinks on their dresses? I don't mind being the villain here."

Amelia managed a strained smile, knowing her friend was capable of doing what she threatened. Mary was the picture of serenity on the outside, but beneath the surface she presented to the world was the heart of a tigress who wouldn't think twice about protecting her friends.

"I'm being silly," Amelia said. "No one had any illusions that this ball would be anything but an opportunity for eligible, unattached women to parade before Lowenbrock in an attempt to capture his interest. But it is one thing to know how they would behave and another to see them in action."

Mary inclined her head to the left, and Amelia turned to see what had captured her friend's attention. She stiffened when she saw that one of the aggressive women was heading in their direction and tried to prepare herself for an unpleasant confrontation.

Amelia should have realized the woman's intent, but she didn't take note of the glass of refreshment in her hand. Fortunately, Mary had and she grasped the other woman's wrist before she could spill the glass's contents over Amelia's dress.

"Careful, *my dear*," Mary said, her voice laced with poisonous sweetness. "It would be a shame if you spilled ratafia all over that *delightful* gown you're wearing. Here, let me take that from you."

Mary whisked the glass away but held it close to the would-be assailant. She maintained her grasp on the woman's wrist with her other hand, however. The grimace on the woman's face made it clear that Mary had added more than a little pressure as a not-so-subtle warning.

When Mary finally released her grip, the woman marched away, casting an angry glare over her shoulder.

"Good heavens, I didn't think someone would actually try that with me."

"Of course they would. You're the most beautiful and intelligent woman in this room, not that any of them care about the latter. You're a threat to their perceived fantasies about winning His Lordship's heart and reigning over this household like a queen."

Amelia shook her head. "I don't even know who that was. I know all the neighbors, and I've never seen her before."

"Probably some distant relation of one of the neighbors who thought to turn this ball to their advantage. If you think things are bad here, it's nothing compared to the season."

Lowenbrock's sisters joined them then. Louisa cast an eye over Amelia and released her breath in a soft sigh. "Thank goodness you're fine. Catherine and I saw what was about to happen, but we were too far away to intervene."

"Honestly," Catherine said, "what did she hope to accomplish? You live here. It would have been an annoyance, but it's not as though you couldn't just go upstairs and change into another gown." She turned to Mary and said, "You should have spilled the drink over her dress."

The group broke out into laughter, and warmth filled Amelia. She'd missed this, being among family and friends. She'd had it for a brief time when she'd gone away to school and met Mary, but it had been years since she'd felt as though she were among family.

Mary looked over Amelia's shoulder, a broad grin spreading over her face. "Don't look now, but your prince is approaching."

Of course Amelia looked over her shoulder. Her heart stuttered when she saw the look on John's face. His attention was centered squarely on her.

When he joined them, he bowed to the group before turning to look at Amelia. "You've been ignoring your duties."

Somehow she kept her mouth from dropping open. "In what way, my lord?"

"You promised to keep me safe from the mamas and the young women who have tried everything in their power to tempt me into compromising them. Instead, I find you over here having fun without me."

His words did much to reassure her. She hadn't wanted to cling to his side, but it was clear he'd been hoping for just that.

She couldn't help needling him. "Are you sure none of them tempted you?"

His soft scoff had the group laughing again. "Next to you, they don't even exist."

Amelia fought the urge to swoon. His soft smile, the way his gray eyes roamed over her face as though he'd been lost and now was saved... If she didn't already love him, she would have fallen under his spell in that moment.

Louisa coughed discreetly into her glove, which was enough to remind them that they weren't alone.

"I think it's time to make our announcement."

Her heart fluttered at the determined look on John's face. He held out his arm, and she took it, the two of them proceeding to the area where the musicians had set up their instruments. He must have already spoken to them because the soft music they played between sets came to an end with a dramatic flourish. The climax of sound drew the attention of several guests. When they saw her and the marquess standing together, waiting for their attention, they spread the word to their less attentive neighbors that something was about to happen.

From the frowns on several of their faces, it was obvious they knew what was coming and they weren't pleased.

The whispers came to a halt, and every eye in the room was trained on them. Amelia had to force back the urge to hide behind John's broad shoulders. She held her hands clasped before her and pasted a neutral smile on her face as she waited for him to begin.

"I would like to thank everyone here for their most gracious welcome. When I was but a soldier in His Majesty's army, I never dreamed I would be returning to England to assume the title of Marquess of Lowenbrock. From what Miss Weston tells me, her uncle was a great man, generous to his tenants and beloved by all in the surrounding neighborhoods. I can only hope to adequately fill the void he left behind when he passed."

Amelia dashed the tear that had formed and threatened to roll down her cheek. John hadn't told her that he'd planned to pay tribute to her uncle, but she shouldn't have been surprised by his words. He hadn't been raised to inherit the title and all that came with it, but she knew her uncle would be proud of him. And relieved that his holdings and tenants were being taken care of.

She looked out at the guests and could see that many were hoping his speech would end there. When he held his hand out to her, she could see the disappointment reflected on their faces. She looked to the man she had agreed to marry and placed her hand in his, unable to quiet the riot of butterflies in her belly. This was all the declaration of their intention to wed that many would need, but John continued, drawing her closer and placing her hand on his arm.

"I would like to announce that Miss Weston has

done me the great honor of accepting my suit and will be the next Marchioness of Lowenbrock."

A polite smattering of applause broke out. John turned to the orchestra and inclined his head. She shouldn't have been surprised when they began to play the opening strains of a waltz.

He led her to the floor, and they took up their positions without another word. They moved together as though they had danced together a thousand times, and after almost a minute, other couples joined them on the floor.

They danced past his friend Cranston, who was smiling down at the woman who'd threatened to ruin her dress, as they joined the waltzing couples. She couldn't help but wonder if he'd partnered with her by design, to keep her occupied during the woman's disappointment. She didn't know the man well, but it seemed as though it was something he would do. She would have to thank him later.

She met John's gaze when he chuckled. "What has amused you?"

He gave his head a rueful shake. "Ashford is going to kill me for not warning him."

"You didn't tell him about our engagement? Surely you don't think he had any romantic intentions toward me. I assure you he has been a gentleman in his behavior."

"No, it isn't that. But the panicked look on his face after I made my announcement and he realized he was now the most eligible bachelor in the room was priceless. I really should have warned him, but I can guarantee he wouldn't have joined us tonight if I had."

Amelia laughed. "You're awful. What is he doing now?"

He inclined his head to one corner, and she saw Ashford deep in conversation with Mary. Finally he held out his arm and Mary took it, following him onto the dance floor.

She had a moment of speculation, wondering if there was something between them, but that was dashed by John's next words.

"I see he's found a shield to hide behind."

She sighed, releasing her disappointment. Of course there was nothing romantic between the two. Their families knew one another, and it made sense that the viscount would seek to hold himself separate from the other women present.

"At least you're no longer in danger of having your head turned by another woman."

John's gaze was deadly serious when he said, "There was never a danger of that happening when you have well and truly ensnared me."

She stopped worrying about everyone else then because the man who held her, drawing her a fraction closer to his body than was seemly, captured her full attention.

She wanted to tell him that she loved him, but she

wouldn't place that burden on him. Men were practical creatures, and it would only disappoint her to hear the words repeated back to her when she wasn't certain if he meant them. But he did care for her, that much was obvious, and it was enough.

ASHFORD WASN'T SURPRISED by his friend's announcement. Not really. What he hadn't expected, however, was the man's secrecy. He'd seen with his own eyes that Evans and Miss Weston were close, but Ashford hadn't realized he'd planned to make an announcement that evening.

Lowenbrock, he corrected himself. He wasn't sure he'd ever get used to the fact that his friend had unexpectedly inherited a marquisate and everything that went along with it. It was the stuff of fairy tales.

Of everyone he'd ever met, Lowenbrock deserved it most. He and Cranston teased him about his chivalrous tendencies, but in truth Ashford admired the man. If he were ever in need of assistance, he'd call on this man first above all others. Cranston was a close second.

Still, it rankled that the man hadn't warned him about what he'd planned for the evening. Likely because Lowenbrock had known he would have stayed away from this infernal event if he even suspected the man intended to announce his betrothal. Because once that happened, all eyes had turned to him and Cranston. But Cranston was only a baron, and so in that moment Ashford had become the most eligible, and sought-after, bachelor present.

Damn the man. Ashford was torn between congratulating him and strangling him, especially after being approached by yet another man who wasted no time in waxing poetic about his eldest daughter's attributes. He'd even come right out and said she would make an ideal viscountess.

Lowenbrock and Miss Weston danced a waltz after the announcement. But the set would come to an end soon, and Ashford didn't miss the way several females had inched closer to him. Too close for his comfort. He wasn't a shy man and had his share of intimate liaisons with the fairer sex, but he wasn't foolish enough to think he could get away with any of his flirtations here. Even the slightest hint that he found any of the women attractive—and how could he not when several of them were almost falling out of their dresses?—would be taken as encouragement to pursue a match. And that was the last thing Ashford wanted. After spending ten years in service, he planned to enjoy his freedom for some time yet before taking on the yoke of marriage.

Lowenbrock's sisters had joined their husbands for the waltz. Cranston, damn his hide, was enjoying the attention and was dancing with one of the younger women. One whose father made no secret of the fact that he wanted a match between his daughter and Ashford, so Cranston no doubt knew he was safe from the family's marital machinations.

He scanned the room and breathed a sigh of relief when he caught sight of Miss Trenton standing off to one side, alone. Her lips were turned up in a fond smile, making no secret of the fact she was happy for her friend. Even if he hadn't known her when she was much younger, the fact she wasn't gazing at him with speculation would have been enough to gain his attention.

She didn't seem to notice him when he stopped next to her.

"Miss Trenton," he said with a bow.

She raised a hand to her chest and frowned at him. "You did that on purpose. I suppose I should consider myself lucky I didn't yelp in surprise."

He smiled. This was the kind of conversation he could handle. "I apologize. It wasn't my intent to catch you unawares."

She turned to look back at the couples dancing to the waltz. "I'm so pleased for Amelia. She cares for Lord Lowenbrock a great deal. They will be happy together."

He'd expected such a statement to be accompanied by a hint of wistfulness, but he detected none. He battled the urge to ask her about her own romantic life. It was none of his business really whether she hoped for a similar outcome as her friend. Society might look down in pity on unwed women, but he'd come across many who would choose independence over an unhappy marriage.

He caught sight of one determined mother heading his way, her young charge in tow. In a panic, he turned back to Miss Trenton. "Save me."

Her gaze met his, her brows drawn together in confusion. "Excuse me?"

"Dance with me and save me from being forced to dance with every young woman here." He inclined his head ever so slightly to the left.

Miss Trenton glanced discreetly in that direction and caught on to his dilemma. She opened the fan dangling at her wrist and covered her mouth so no one else would see the wicked smile she shared with him. "Surely you can do better than that."

He refrained from scowling at her, knowing that any indication on his part that he wasn't enjoying this conversation would have the matchmaking mama barging between the two of them.

"Would you do me the great honor of joining me in this dance?"

"I don't know. What will the others think since you haven't danced once this evening? And a waltz, no less."

She'd noticed that? One corner of his mouth quirked upward. "They would believe that yours is the only attention worth having."

Miss Trenton's smile was genuine, her eyes

dancing with merriment. "Well done, my lord." She gave a small curtsy and took the arm he offered.

They joined the other couples waltzing, and he breathed a sigh of relief as he took Miss Trenton into his arms.

"I owe you a debt of gratitude," he said, ignoring the urge to bring her closer.

CHAPTER 32

IT WAS LATE WHEN AMELIA retired to her chambers. Or rather very early since it was technically the next day. Overall, she'd enjoyed the evening despite the speculation about her living arrangements at Brock Manor. Speculation that only intensified after the announcement of their betrothal. She hadn't missed the glances at her midsection as many no doubt wondered whether she'd trapped him into declaring himself.

Still, John's sisters and their husbands made it clear that they'd taken her firmly under their wing, and no one dared breathe a word of censure to her face.

She hadn't wanted the evening to end as she'd danced with all her well-wishers, and to her surprise there'd been more than a few. But all too soon the music ended and guests began to say their goodbyes.

Louisa, Catherine, and Mary had whisked her away, telling her that since she wasn't yet the lady of the manor, she needn't stand by John's side as people made their way from the ballroom. And truth be told, she hadn't wanted to subject herself to the glares of her thwarted rivals up close.

She'd let them take her away, disappointed that she wouldn't be able to say good night to her betrothed. John's sisters had flanked her as they exited the ballroom and made their way upstairs to their bedrooms. A show meant to send the message that she was being properly chaperoned even if that wasn't strictly true.

Her maid was already waiting in her chambers, and it had taken the woman little time to take down Amelia's hair and help her out of her ball gown.

Amelia took one final turn about her bedroom, knowing that soon the excitement of the evening would wear off and she'd finally be able to fall asleep. She'd just removed her dressing gown and was about to make the attempt when a soft rap at her bedroom door had her stopping in her tracks.

Her pulse immediately leaped in anticipation, but she chastised herself for being silly. John wouldn't visit her that night, not when there were so many guests.

She opened the door a crack, thrilled to discover she was wrong.

Giving her head a small shake, she stepped back and waited for him to enter. When he locked the door behind her, anticipation surged through her veins.

"I didn't expect to see you tonight. I thought you wanted to safeguard my reputation."

He reached for her and dragged her into his arms. "After announcing our betrothal, this could very well be the last time we're able to be together for some time."

She twined her arms around his neck, pressing her body against his. "We could designate a special place to meet. Besides, aren't your sisters planning to leave tomorrow?"

"Yes, and tongues will wag unless we find someone to become your companion. Perhaps your friend Mary?"

The idea appealed to her. She hadn't seen Mary since leaving school, their friendship taking place via correspondence over the past nine years.

"I'll ask her tomorrow. How long do you think she'll have to stay?"

"Much as I would love to leave tomorrow and head to London for a special license, that will only start rumors about the haste of our nuptials. Added to the fact we've been living under the same roof for a few months now…"

"Our neighbors are likely to jump to the *right* conclusion," she finished.

His lips twisted. "Yes. But I would save you from such gossip if I could."

"I don't mind, but I must say that I welcome the opportunity to spend more time with Mary. I'm sure she won't insist on moving into my room to keep me chaste until we're wed."

"I hope not!" He touched his mouth to hers but pulled away after a moment.

She let out a frustrated sigh. "It's July now. Would autumn do? September or October?"

"We can read the banns and go about this business the traditional way."

"Did you see all those disappointed faces when you made the announcement?"

"No. I scarce noticed anyone but you."

Amelia feigned a swoon. "If I hadn't already accepted your proposal, my lord, that announcement would have been enough to convince me."

He answered her with a kiss.

She was already in her nightdress, but he caught up to her in quick order, and finally they were together in her bed. Unlike that first night, there was no tentative fumbling on her part, no caution on his. Perhaps it was the time they had been apart, or his concern they might not be able to make love again in the foreseeable future, but he took possession of her body with a confidence that had her trembling with desire.

Her heart was racing when he thrust inside her, and she reached her peak almost immediately. He was relentless, however, continuing until she reached another climax before pulling out of her and spending himself outside her body. She clung to him, a fine sheen of sweat coating her body, as she waited for her breathing to return to normal. She and John would be husband and wife within three months, and when that day arrived, he would be able to find his pleasure within her body. She couldn't wait until they no longer needed to be so careful about preventing pregnancy.

He placed a hand under her chin and tilted her face to his. "September. I'll die if I have to wait any longer than that to fully claim you."

She settled back against him, contentment settling over her. Yes, he did care for her, perhaps even loved her. Even if he never said the words, she knew the truth.

CHAPTER 33

*I*T WAS STILL DARK when John woke. If there was one habit that had stayed with him from his many years in the army, it was his ability to survive on only a few hours of sleep. He wasn't sure he'd ever experience a full night of uninterrupted sleep again. At least the nightmares had lessened in intensity as the months passed.

He glanced over at Amelia. At some point she'd shifted in her sleep and now lay with her back to him. She'd raised the sheet to cover her upper body, but his penchant for tossing back his sheets had bared her back. His eyes traveled down the long line of her spine, which disappeared beneath the bedclothes that still covered her hips. He wanted to wake her, bury his hands in the wild curls that spread out over her pillow, and take her again.

But he couldn't risk getting caught in her

bedchamber. He'd already risked having her fall with child. He'd taken precautions, but from what he'd been told, it wasn't a guaranteed method of preventing pregnancy. He shouldn't have come here tonight, but he couldn't stand the idea of not having one last night with her before he was forced to keep his distance.

He dressed quickly, frowning as he thought about the two months that needed to pass before they could wed to stanch the gossip. But he'd lived through worse. Soon enough, they would be married and would never again be separated.

Perhaps he should leave the estate and take up rooms at the nearest inn.

He glanced once more at Amelia, trying to paint a picture of her in his mind to carry him through the next two months. When he finally dragged his eyes away, his gaze fell on the stack of papers on her bedside table. The curtains hadn't been drawn, and the moonlight streaming through the windows meant he could peek at what she'd written.

He knew he shouldn't, but he rose from the bed, scooped up the pages, and walked over to the window.

And still he hesitated. He wasn't sure why since she hoped to have the book published. Everyone would then be able to read it, including him. And she had told him he would be able to read it.

He glanced down at the top sheet and began to

read. Confusion swept through him when he realized this wasn't the beginning of the book. Instead, it was a list of things he'd said to her over the period of their acquaintance. He flipped through the first few pages and found notes on what he'd worn at times and how he'd looked at her. His heart froze when he reached the last phrase of the list—*John and I make love for the first time.*

Perhaps this was a journal of sorts, a way for her to keep track of everything that happened between them. He didn't want to turn to the next page, but at that point he couldn't stop. He had to make sure these were simple recollections on her part and not something much, much worse.

He turned the page and began to read when he saw CHAPTER ONE written at the top. And stopped when he realized it was a fictionalized retelling of what had happened that night at the tavern. Oh, the heroine was different, and Amelia hinted at a character backstory that was vastly different from her own. One of a woman reduced to poverty and who had no alternative but to accept work that was far below her station. But when a man stepped in to save her from the unwelcome advances of one of the patrons, she'd captured him in some detail.

A gasp from behind told him that Amelia had woken. Careful, lest he give in to the impulse to do something childish, he shuffled the pages so they were in order again, using the time to rein in his anger. He returned to her bed and deposited the manuscript on the bedside table.

She didn't speak as he began to dress. When he'd donned his trousers and shirt, he turned to face her again.

One hand held the bedsheet to her chest while the other was curled against her mouth. Most of her color had drained from her face.

"I see now why you didn't want me to read this."

She made a sound of distress and scrambled from the bed. He waited, hating how much he still wanted her as he watched her slip on her nightdress and scramble around the side of the bed to face him.

"It isn't what it appears—"

"Really? Because what it looks like is you wrote about me in your novel."

She winced. "At first, yes, but when I started writing that book, I didn't know who you were. You were just a handsome stranger who'd acted gallantly, and I couldn't shake the certainty that you would make the perfect hero. Or at least my impression of the character based on those few moments of interaction we'd had."

He hadn't realized his jaw was clenched so tightly until he barked out a short laugh. "Really? And what about the notes you took, capturing my very words after I arrived at Brock Manor? Now I know why you were constantly taking out that notebook and jotting notes whenever we were together."

"I planned to change all that. I got carried away. You were the perfect hero and…" She spread her hands in defeat. "It was foolish, but I will be taking all that out."

"Is that the reason you wanted to make love to me that day? So you could gather more *research* for your novel?" The way she flinched at his words told him his guess had been correct. "Tell me, Amelia, are you taking those things out because it's the right thing to do? Or because I caught you at your game?"

She was trembling, and he hated that he had to curb the desire to take her into his arms and soothe her hurt. He was the injured party here, not her.

"That was a list of things I need to go change when I edit the book. I was swept up in everything that was happening between us and failed to place proper distance between my feelings and what I was trying to capture for the story. But I *will* be making those changes."

When she started to step forward, he held up a hand to stop her. "We need some time apart so cooler heads can prevail. I have to leave before anyone finds me in your bedchamber."

He was no longer that young man who'd run away without his family's knowledge and joined the army. He wanted—no, he *needed*—to sort out this mess with Amelia. But not right now. He couldn't speak about this while he wasn't in control of his emotions. He needed to wait until the initial shock had worn off.

She locked her gaze onto his for several long moments, during which he couldn't move. Her shoulders slumped, and she looked down at the floor. "I can break the engagement—"

"No. Absolutely not. I made a promise, and I intend to keep it." He took a step toward the door but paused before leaving. "Everyone except Miss Trenton will be leaving later today. I'm sure we'll find the time to talk about this then."

With that, he turned and left before he could say or do anything that would make the situation worse.

CHAPTER 34

*S*HE COULDN'T GO BACK TO SLEEP after he
left. She stared at the pages that had
damned her in John's eyes as she tried to decide
whether she was scared, upset with herself, or angry
with him. She decided that all three together were an
adequate description of the emotions roiling within
her as she set about removing any evidence that the
man she loved had been in her bedroom. She was
certain the staff already knew about just how far their
physical relationship had progressed, but that didn't
mean she was comfortable advertising the fact.

She'd been careless and more than a little foolish
in her interactions with John. She should have been
honest with him from the start, first about that night
in the tavern and then about the subject of her book.
She knew now that he wouldn't have condemned her
if she'd explained that she was having difficulty sepa-

rating her feelings for him from what she wanted her characters to experience as their relationship progressed. It wasn't her fault that he was so witty and that she'd been tempted to use some of his observations in her novel. But she'd taken it too far.

She hadn't lied when she told him that the list he'd found were instances where there was too much of a similarity between the character she was writing and the man she loved. She'd planned to eradicate most of those passages and soften others. It was fine to take inspiration from someone, but something else entirely to use them in such a manner without their permission.

But he could have stayed and talked this out with her. How was she supposed to get through the rest of the day knowing he was too angry to speak to her? A small part of her couldn't help but wonder if she was acting the hypocrite since she'd kept things from him as well. Honestly, she didn't know whether to be angrier at John or at herself.

He still wants to marry you.

After taking one last look about the room to ensure he hadn't left behind any of his clothing, she threw herself back on the bed and stared up at the ceiling.

Did he want to marry her, or did he feel obligated to marry her?

Her thoughts reeled as she considered the very real possibility that he was behaving in the exact same manner as he'd done that first night when he'd saved her from that man who'd wanted more than a drink from her. Society dictated that John couldn't end their betrothal without leaving her reputation in tatters... and, if truth be told, branding himself something of a scoundrel. He would overcome that in time, but she wouldn't. And if she knew only one thing about the man she loved, it was that he always tried to do the right thing.

But she could end the betrothal and save the reputations of them both.

All society will see is the fact that the two of you have been living under the same roof for three months.

She wanted to tell that small voice with its unfortunate truths to stay quiet.

You could leave and stay with one of his sisters.

She closed her eyes as soon as that thought occurred to her because she realized it was the course of action she needed to take. John was concerned about her reputation—he'd said as much. But would Mary's presence be enough to quiet the rumors that had no doubt started to spread the moment John had announced their betrothal? She'd seen the annoyance and the jealousy on the faces of some of the young women present, but she'd also seen the speculative look in the expressions of their parents. In particular, their fathers.

No, she couldn't remain under the same roof as him. He'd said that he wanted to wed in September, which was two months from now. If she left Brock Manor, some of that speculation would disappear. The two months apart would also give John enough time to decide if he'd changed his mind about ending their betrothal.

Her heart clenched at the thought, but it was the right thing to do. Many other women wouldn't think twice about entrapping their target and forcing them to the altar, but she wasn't one of them. She'd come to terms with the fact that John might not love her, but he did care for her. And until a short while ago, she'd made him happy. She couldn't live the rest of her life with him if he started to look at her with distrust instead of affection.

John's sisters had been kind to her, treating her as though she were already one of the family. They wouldn't turn down her request, especially since they, too, wouldn't want a scandal. She knew that the next two months would be difficult, but hopefully their time apart would give John the time he needed to decide whether he could forgive her lie of omission.

Whether she'd be able to forgive herself, however, was another matter entirely.

CHAPTER 35

JOHN FORCED HIMSELF to act as though everything were normal. It had been a decade since he'd left home to enlist, and he hoped he'd learned how to conceal his emotions in that time. If his sisters suspected he was trying to hide his inner turmoil, they said nothing.

His friends, however, were another matter. It was impossible to miss the concerned looks that passed between Ashford and Cranston. They tried to pull him aside several times before their departures that morning, but John managed to avoid their questions. Fortunately, they didn't press the matter. All too soon, he was standing outside and bidding them goodbye.

Cranston clapped him on the shoulder. "I look forward to receiving your wedding invitation. Will it be soon?"

John knew what he was asking—did he need to

wed Amelia quickly to cover up the fact that she was already with child?

He shook his head. "It will be in the fall. We'll let you know when we've finalized our plans."

Ashford gave him a formal bow. "We look forward to it. Miss Weston seems to be a fine woman. I'm sure the two of you will be happy together."

John nodded by way of reply, knowing that Ashford was right. He and Amelia *would* be happy together once this matter was behind them.

He watched his friends enter the carriage they'd shared on the way to Yorkshire and set off on the long trip back to London.

It hadn't taken long for him to regret leaving Amelia that morning. He should have stayed and talked matters out with her. She'd wanted to explain and he hadn't given her the opportunity, allowing his sense of betrayal to color his actions. As soon as his sisters and their husbands left, he planned to remedy the situation.

He was sitting in the drawing room with his two brothers-in-law before their departure. Once, he'd disliked the Marquess of Overlea on principle, but he'd been young then and unable to see beyond that hatred. Now he had nothing but respect for the man.

He would miss his family when they left, but in that moment he couldn't wait for them to depart. He had yet to see Amelia that morning. She was probably saying her own goodbyes to his sisters. And then he could finally be alone with her again. Amelia's friend would still be in residence, but it would be much easier to steal his betrothed away from one guest than from seven.

John took a sandwich from the tea tray before him and demolished it while Overlea and Kerrick discussed where they should stop for the night.

John fixed his gaze on Kerrick, giving in to his curiosity. "You'll have to tell me the story of your courtship of Catherine. She hinted at some near heartbreak there."

Kerrick winced. "Yes. Maybe one day I'll tell you about it. We'll need something more than tea, however."

Overlea leaned back in his chair. "I'm glad you're happily situated here. Louisa never stopped worrying about you over the years, and then when you left London shortly after your arrival…" He lifted a shoulder. "She was concerned you'd be lonely."

John could only shake his head. "Louisa fell into the role of acting as mother to me and Catherine when our mother died."

"That might have been true once, but she's been content to let go of her fretting since our children were born. But she was quite put out with me for not chasing you down and forcing you to return."

John shook his head. He might not have left Brock Manor in the middle of the night, but his behavior toward Amelia last night had been just as selfish.

"That definitely wasn't the best decision I've ever made, but I don't regret enlisting. If I had it to do over, I would wait to take my leave instead of disappearing."

"You needed to become your own man. And much as you hated me, I do understand that."

"Catherine was also worried, but she understood your perspective. She's been known to take a few risks herself. I almost dread what she'll want to do when the children are grown and out of the house."

John could well remember the trouble Catherine used get into when she was younger. Now that he thought about it, it was no wonder Louisa had constantly worried about them. He raised his cup of tea in salute. "Well, here's to happy endings. Soon I'll be joining you in wedded bliss."

Overlea and Kerrick didn't say anything, but from their knowing smirks, it was clear they suspected he and Amelia had already consummated the physical side of their relationship.

The moment was interrupted by the sound of a throat clearing. They turned to find Louisa standing in the doorway, hands on her hips. "Isn't it a little early to be drinking?"

"Yes, mother," John said, standing.

Overlea and Kerrick rose as well. Louisa crossed her arms and glared at them. Catherine popped into position next to her and shook her head.

"You can't win," Overlea said. "And since

becoming a mother, your sister has become adept at making one wither with a single glance."

"Well, my cup has tea in it," Kerrick said, bending down to grab his cup and raise it into view. "I can't speak for these other characters."

Overlea lifted his cup as well, and with a sigh, so did John.

"Very good," Louisa said, smiling warmly at her husband.

John wondered if he was so transparent in his affection whenever he looked at Amelia. He probably was. "Will you be joining us? I can ask for a fresh pot of tea."

Catherine shook her head. "We had something to eat with Amelia and Mary. I fear it's time now for us to depart."

They all stepped out into the hallway, and John couldn't help but think back to his family's small cottage. They never would have all fit in that hallway. It was still impossible to believe just how much their lives had changed.

He looked toward the stairs and then down the hall that led to the back of the house, wondering what was keeping Amelia. She wouldn't miss saying goodbye to his family.

He engulfed his sisters in a hug.

First Catherine, who whispered in his ear, "You did well! I like Amelia very much. I look forward to having her in our family."

Louisa held on a little longer, and when he finally pulled back, she dashed a tear from her eye.

He examined her expression. "Still worried about me?"

Louisa shook her head. "No, I'm happy and relieved and disappointed that I have to leave so soon. But I miss the children."

"We'll see you again in a couple of months for the wedding." He squeezed her hand and stepped back.

Her smile widened. "I'll do everything I can to aid Amelia with the preparations until you can join us."

Her words caused a small frisson of unease to unfurl in his abdomen. He was about to ask her to explain further, but movement out of the corner of his eye had him turning to look at the stairs. Amelia and Mary were descending, the latter saying something that amused Amelia. But her smile was reserved.

He couldn't stop staring as she descended the stairs and joined them and he tried to discern what was happening. He wanted to demand an explanation from Louisa, but there were too many people crowded into the hallway, their voices filling the space. And if he was being honest, he couldn't shake the irrational fear that if he looked away, the woman he loved would disappear forever.

When Amelia's gaze met his, he could see the wariness reflected in their depths. He needed to apologize for his selfish behavior and set things right with her as soon as possible.

One by one, his sisters and brothers-in-law exited the house. Amelia's friend trailed behind them.

With one last glance at Amelia, Mary said, "I'll see you outside."

"Is your friend leaving today as well? I thought you were going to ask her to stay."

Amelia met his gaze and inclined her head toward the drawing room.

Dread settled over him as he followed. "We can speak after everyone leaves."

Amelia took a deep breath and looked at him, her shoulders pulled back and her fingers entwined at her waist. "I'm going with them."

He could only stare at her for several moments, wondering if he'd heard her correctly. Finally he shook his head. "No—"

"Yes. I have to go. You wanted to guard my reputation, and this is how we do that. I've spoken to your eldest sister and she agrees. I'll be staying with her, which will give you time to decide whether you've changed your mind about our future."

"I haven't. I've already told you that. We *will* be getting married."

He reached for her, but she took a step back. His arms dropped to his side, emptiness beginning to fill his heart.

"I do want that, but you don't trust me. You accused me of using you as research."

"I was shocked, and my accusations weren't without reason at the time. Surely you can see that."

Her eyes shone, and he had the horrible suspicion that she was holding back tears. "I do, which is why we need some time apart. I let my fear rule me. I should have been honest with you from the start, and for that I am sorry. But you need some time to decide whether you can learn to trust me again, because I won't accept anything less than that in a marriage. I don't want you to marry me just because you feel you have to save my reputation."

"That's not why I want to marry you."

"I hope not." She turned and walked out into the hallway.

"Don't go, Amelia."

She didn't reply as she took her hat and gloves from the butler and followed her friend outside.

Numbness filled him as he followed. He wanted to grab hold of Amelia and keep her at his side, but she'd outmaneuvered him. The horrible thought occurred to him that perhaps it was she who had changed her mind.

But no, she wasn't that good of an actress. He'd seen clearly that she was nervous around him when they first met and for some time afterward. He knew now that was because she hadn't been comfortable with the half-truths she'd told him. But the time they'd spent together since becoming intimate—that was genuine. He'd seen the real Amelia, and he had no intention of letting her go.

He shook hands again with his brothers-in-law and allowed his sisters to draw him into another hug.

"Take good care of her," he said when his oldest sister pulled back.

"I will. Come to London soon so we can finalize the wedding arrangements."

He nodded. "I'll send word."

Amelia smiled as she dipped into a curtsy, but it didn't reach her eyes. He didn't miss the sympathetic look Miss Trenton cast his way before she followed Amelia into the carriage.

Finally, when everyone was inside, the carriages pulled away. His sisters waved to him from the windows, but Amelia, who was leaving with Louisa and Overlea, kept her gaze averted.

He took several deep breaths as he wrestled with the urge to demand that his own carriage be prepared so he could follow them. He stood in silence, watching as the carriages drew farther away. He vowed this wouldn't be the last time he saw Amelia. He knew that if she desired it, Markham would help her disappear into the country somewhere.

He wouldn't let that happen. He would find a way to prove that he loved and trusted her.

The irony of the situation wasn't lost on him. All those years ago, he'd been the one to run away when he couldn't deal with the way things had turned out with his family. But now he was staying and was forced to watch the one person who meant more to him than any other threaten to slip away.

He'd acted in haste and youthful anger then. There was no anger now, neither on his part nor Amelia's. But there was hurt. He'd give her the time she needed, but not too much time. Then he'd head to London and make sure she returned home with him, this time as his wife. He couldn't imagine a future without Amelia by his side, and he *would* make that happen.

CHAPTER 36

*H*E LASTED ONE WEEK at Brock Manor before the quiet and emptiness threatened to drive him insane. Mrs. Brambles seemed to sense his loneliness, attaching herself to his side and finding a comfortable place to sleep in whatever room he occupied. Or perhaps she missed Amelia as well. Cats were supposed to be aloof creatures, but that wasn't the case with the gray tabby who shadowed him after Amelia's departure.

On the morning of the seventh day, he turned to Mrs. Brambles, who was doing an admirable job of pretending to sleep in the middle of his bed while he paced the floor of his bedroom.

"I'm going to get her back."

Mrs. Brambles opened her eyes, fixed her gazed on him for several seconds, and then gave a soft, urgent mewl. *Why are you still standing there then?*

"Right." John held out his hand for Mrs. Brambles. She rubbed her cheek against it, offering her support for his course of action, before settling back into a ball. Her purr of contentment was all the approval he needed.

He'd wanted to jump onto a horse right away, but the trip to London would be too long on horseback, even stopping to change mounts at posting inns along the way. In the end, he paced for another hour while the carriage was readied and Oliver packed a small trunk with what he deemed to be essentials.

But Amelia was the only thing he needed.

With a quick reminder to the staff to look after Mrs. Brambles, John swung into the carriage. If he'd thought the trip out to the estate was long with Markham insisting they stop at every inn along the way, he soon realized that was nothing when compared to this one.

The sun had already set when his carriage reached the Overlea town house in London. The door swung open when he approached.

"Good evening, my lord," Overlea's butler said with a small bow.

"Sommers. I hope my sister is at home?"

"Of course. Would you care to wait in the drawing room while I announce your visit?"

John nodded and headed in that direction. Louisa had always been organized, and he had no doubt she would have asked the staff to prepare the bedroom he'd used when he was in residence the last time he'd stayed. He couldn't stop thinking about the fact that Amelia was here somewhere and prayed she would come down with his sister. Or instead of her.

"John."

He'd been pacing, and at the sound of his sister's voice, he turned to face her. Disappointment crashed over him when he saw she was alone.

She moved to the settee, patting the seat next to her. He joined her, letting out a harsh breath.

"I didn't know when to expect you. You didn't send word, and Amelia refused to discuss your relationship. Did something happen between the two of you?"

As always, Louisa couldn't stop mothering him. When he was younger, he'd chafed under her concerned gaze, but today he welcomed it. Just one more way in which he'd changed over the years.

"It seems I cannot stop from acting first and reconsidering afterward. I fear I've made a mess of my life."

Louisa tilted her head, gazing at him in confusion. "I don't think that's true. Amelia is a wonderful young woman. You chose wisely with her. It's clear to anyone who sees the two of you together that you care about one another."

"I love her, but I don't know if she feels the same."

Louisa let out a soft sigh. "You didn't tell her."

"I wanted to… I was going to, but then we had an

argument. Before I could apologize for assuming the worst, she'd made plans to leave." He ran a hand through his already unkempt hair. "I didn't know she was leaving with you that morning."

Louisa placed a hand on his knee, squeezing it briefly. "I thought something was wrong that morning, but I assumed it was because you didn't want her to leave. Amelia told us that it would curb gossip if she left Yorkshire. I didn't know she hadn't spoken to you about her plans."

John stood and paced away from his sister. "She didn't." He turned to face her again. "Can you have a footman fetch her? I can't wait a moment longer to see her." He shook his head, realizing he didn't want to wait even that long to see her again. "No, just tell me where she is right now and I'll go speak to her."

"She isn't here."

He tried to quell the panic that rose within him at her statement. It had almost killed him to wait one week, and now that he was in London, he didn't want to wait a moment longer.

"Is she at Catherine's home? Please tell me they're in residence here and not at their country seat." He turned to look at the tall clock that stood in the corner of the room, wondering if he could head out again tonight.

"No, she's not there either. She isn't staying with us. She's staying with your solicitor, Mr. Markham.

Apparently she thought it would inconvenience us to stay here."

John didn't hold back his slight snort at the ridiculous thought. Louisa *loved* mothering people. She'd never be put out by having Amelia stay with her and Overlea.

"Tell me she left the address. I don't think I can wait until tomorrow to call at his office."

"Of course. I'll fetch it for you."

She left the room and was back a minute later, but every second of delay felt like an eternity. He'd begun pacing again while he waited.

He took the folded piece of paper she handed him and glanced at the address. It wasn't nearby, but he was relieved that it was in a respectable area of town. He gave his head a slight shake. Of course it was. Markham wouldn't live in one of the unsavory areas.

"Say something," Louisa prodded when he'd been silent for too long.

He opened his mouth to do just that, then closed it again. Finally he said, "I don't know what to do."

"What you need to do is find that woman and tell her that you love her. That you're done acting like a stubborn fool."

He wanted to protest, but his sister had always possessed an infuriating talent for being in the right. It was one of the things that used to annoy him to no end.

"I accused her of using me." He laughed, the

sound bitter to his own ears. He shook his head. "I need to go to her."

Louisa smiled at him, fondness evident in her gaze. "Don't let me keep you any longer."

He took a step toward the door, then turned back to her. He pulled Louisa into a quick hug, one which she returned with a fierceness he wouldn't have thought possible.

When he released her and took a step back, she shooed him away. "You mustn't tarry on my behalf. We can speak again later."

He dropped a kiss on her cheek and strode from the house. He needed to find his future wife and beg her forgiveness for ever doubting her.

CHAPTER 37

*W*ITH NOTHING TO DO since arriving in London, Amelia devoted herself to finishing her book. She'd gone through all the notations she'd made where the hero of her novel was too similar to John and changed them. The book was finished, but the manuscript was riddled with areas where she'd crossed out entire passages and inserted spare pages with the text that would replace those scenes. Then came the task of copying the final version in preparation for submission to a publisher.

But she hadn't changed the opening scene, when the heroine was threatened with assault at the tavern where she was working as a barmaid and the hero jumped in to rescue her. That scene was vital to the entire plot. Other than John's two friends, who'd been present when she had first met him, no one would realize the events depicted in that scene had actually taken place.

She spent her days completing the task of copying the pages, allowing herself to get pulled into her heroine's story and all the struggles she faced. She tried not to think about what would come next. The idea of sending the manuscript to a publisher and having it accepted was her dream, but she wasn't ready to take that step. Not until she and John could reconcile. She wouldn't even dwell on the possibility that the book could be rejected.

As she did every day since her arrival in London, she forced herself to rise early and have breakfast with Mr. Markham. She could have stayed with one of John's sisters—both had offered her a place in their homes—but she couldn't help but worry that John might change his mind about marrying her.

The kindly solicitor departed for his office at the customary hour, leaving Amelia to return to her bedroom and continue her work. Sighing, she sat before the dressing table she'd turned into a desk, picked up her quill, and prepared the tip with care. Copying over a manuscript was tedious work, made only worse when she hurried and left a smear of ink on the page since she'd have to start over with a fresh page and copy the words anew.

As she had every day since arriving in town, Amelia wished she'd been able to bring Mrs. Brambles with her. But the cat had never liked being confined during carriage rides, and so she'd left her at the estate where she was no doubt happy basking in John's company. She knew very well how the cat felt and wished she, too, was back in Yorkshire with the two of them. Pushing back her doubts about the future, she dipped her quill into the inkwell and continued from where she'd left off the day before.

It was late when Mr. Markham returned. He called out a greeting as he passed her bedroom before heading to his room to change for dinner. With a sigh, Amelia set aside her work and made her way downstairs to wait for him.

She had just reached the front room when a knock at the front door had her pausing. Curious, she waited for the butler to answer the door. She didn't know why, but something within her knew who it would be.

The front door swung open, and her heart threatened to stop when she saw John standing there.

She drank in the sight of him. His pale hair was disarrayed, reminding her of long, languorous nights spent together. Their gazes met and held, his gray eyes dark as though a storm brewed within them.

His clothing hung loose on his large frame, and she realized he'd lost weight even though they'd only been apart one week. It appeared he'd been as miserable as she, and her heart soared with hope. It took an inordinate amount of effort not to fly into his arms.

She told Markham's butler that John could enter and then moved into the front room. The sound of his steps on the wooden floors told her he followed. She turned and faced him, her throat dry.

When he didn't speak, she managed to whisper, "Mr. Markham will be down shortly for dinner. Should I ask for another place to be set at the table?"

One corner of his mouth tilted up. "I'm not here to see Markham, although I won't say no to dinner. Traveling nonstop from Yorkshire can work up quite an appetite."

He came closer, stopping when he was almost within reach. She had the impression of voices sounding in the hallway—no doubt the butler informing Mr. Markham of their visitor—but she couldn't tear her eyes from the man before her to see if anyone witnessed their interaction. She didn't care.

"I'm so sorry—"

They both spoke at the same time. Unable to hold back any longer, Amelia flew into his arms with a soft sound of relief. John gathered her to his chest, solid and warm, and she never wanted to leave.

The man she loved was the one to pull back first. Amelia wanted to protest, but then she saw Mr. Markham standing in the doorway, his grin wide. With a nod, he turned and left the two of them to their reconciliation.

John stared down at her, his arms around her

waist, hers gripping his shoulders. "It seems an eternity since I last held you."

Amelia burrowed into another embrace. "It *has* been an eternity."

He kept her against him with one arm, the other moving along the line of her spine. From top to bottom, then starting over, much as he stroked Mrs. Brambles. Somehow Amelia managed not to purr.

She glanced up at him again after several long moments passed. "I should have talked to you about my book long before you found it. You inspired the hero, yes, but I'd already decided on the storyline before I realized you were Lowenbrock. You were just a handsome stranger who'd rescued me that night in the tavern."

He opened his mouth to reply, but she quieted him by placing the fingers of one hand over his mouth. "Those notes you found..." She took in a shuddering breath and moved her hand to thread her fingers in the hair at his nape. "I had finished going through the book and making notes of everything I needed to change because the hero had become much too similar to you. You were never *research* but inspiration. At first it was difficult for me to separate the hero in my book from the real you. Because honestly, how could you be so ridiculously handsome and gallant and... Well, and everything a hero *should* be. But I realized I couldn't share everything about you in that way. And so I made a list of everything that needed to change."

She held her breath, waiting for his reply. Desperately praying he would understand.

"But not the happy ending, I hope? Or am I wrong in thinking the book ends happily?"

She muffled a sob and was about to reply, but this time John quieted her with a quick, hard kiss.

"It's my turn now. First, I want to apologize for jumping to the worst possible conclusion."

"Given how we met, I don't blame you. And then I kept our first meeting a secret for so long—"

He gave her a small shake. "No, don't blame yourself. I was still reeling from the realization that I was in love with you, and then when I found those notes listing things I'd said and done…" He shook his head. "You were right—I should have trusted you. It seems to be a pattern in my life that I run away, convinced I am correct in my indignation, instead of staying to listen. I did that all those years ago with Louisa when she accepted Overlea's proposal of marriage, and I did it again with you. But I promise to do better next time. And if I do repeat that pattern, you have my permission to track me down and give me a stern talking-to about assumptions. But please don't ever leave me again, and never doubt my love for you."

Could he feel her racing heart where her chest was pressed against his own? "I love you too. More than I ever thought possible."

He stared down at her, and she knew he could see the truth of her words on her face because she was done keeping secrets from him. She loved this man, and she wanted the whole world to know it.

He kissed her then, and she could almost feel his heart in the soft caress of his mouth against hers.

CHAPTER 38

1817
Yorkshire

HER BOOK WAS A ROUSING SUCCESS, far beyond Amelia's wildest imaginings. The story of a woman who'd fallen on desperate times and found love in the unlikeliest of places, it struck a chord with many. Her publisher had rushed to get it into print, taking a gamble that had paid off. And now apparently people were trying to figure out the author's real identity.

Amelia lowered the newspaper she was reading with a loud sigh. Several names had been considered, but it appeared no one believed the author was a woman.

She stroked Mrs. Brambles's head where the cat had curled next to her on the drawing room settee.

Amelia should be glad her identity wasn't in danger of being exposed, especially after reading the assertions that no proper lady would be indelicate enough to write about the emotions she'd portrayed. She'd changed the hero enough that no one knew he'd been modeled on a real person, but the hypocrisy of the reading public confounded her. Most of the book's readers were women, so why was it so hard to believe that one of their sex could have written it?

She heard the slight murmur of voices in the hallway, announcing that her husband had returned from his morning ride. John stepped into the room and she met his gaze, wincing when she saw his slight frown. He'd seen the discarded newspaper on her lap, and she knew he worried she'd be upset at not receiving the praise he said she was due.

She lifted one shoulder in a small shrug and folded the pages before placing the newspaper on the low table before the settee. "You can hardly blame me for being curious."

He lowered himself next to her and reached across her lap to stroke their pampered tabby on the top of her head before leaning back to look at her. After several moments of silence, he reached into a pocket of his deep brown topcoat and retrieved a letter. "This came for you from your publisher."

She took the letter with a hint of trepidation and broke the seal. "They can't be asking about the next book. I've only just started it."

John placed an arm around her shoulders as she scanned the brief letter. She'd confessed to him her fear that her second book wouldn't be as well received as the first. He hadn't offered meaningless words of comfort—it was highly unlikely, after all, that all her books would be released to the same fanfare. But he had told her that he believed in her and that if her fears proved true, he knew she wouldn't give up and would try again with another book and then another. His unwavering support had given her the confidence to start writing again.

Her concern turned to joy, and she handed the letter back to her husband. "They're planning to do a second printing."

His smile widened, matching her grin. But there was something in his eyes that hinted at uncertainty.

She searched his features, trying to decipher what could be troubling him, before asking, "What is the matter?"

John gazed down at the letter again. "They're going to print again next month with a larger number of copies."

She didn't care that she was beaming. It seemed she would never stop smiling when she thought about the success of her book. "I'm sure they're hoping for an increase in sales given all the young debutantes that are even now descending on London."

John gave an exaggerated shudder. "Thank heavens I was able to avoid that scene! Not that I won't be content to escort you to any event you wish to attend, but it is unsettling being at the center of all that attention. I'm still recovering from the ball we hosted last summer."

"Are you nervous about Parliament then? Your brothers-in-law will support you."

He shook his head. "I'm not worried about that. But I was thinking… when we arrive in town, we can speak to your publisher about having your name printed as the author on this second edition. I know they didn't think it was a good idea, but I hate to see your accomplishments go unacknowledged."

Warmth spread through her at the earnest expression on his face. She'd known he still felt guilty about the way he'd reacted all those months before, but it amazed her that he would suggest such a thing. They knew what would happen if the public learned just who had written that book. Their every movement would be observed, and speculation about their private life would be rife just as he was making his first appearance in the House of Lords. They'd survive the scandal, of course, but the next few months would be unbearable, and her husband was very much a private man.

She settled deeper into his embrace.

"Maybe one day. But for now I am content knowing that my writing is being read and enjoyed. And if I'm being honest, I rather enjoy the speculation."

"You're not upset that everyone is intent on giving credit to someone else? People who might gain unearned notoriety from your efforts?"

She shook her head. "No. Truthfully, I'm sure the mystery has helped with sales. Once that mystery is gone…" She lifted one shoulder in a casual shrug.

"Still, it hardly seems just—"

She placed a hand over his lips. "For now, I have another creation that will require most of my attention."

She could tell he still had his doubts, but he raised one of her hands and dropped a kiss onto her palm. "Your new book is going well?"

"That and…" She turned his hand that still grasped hers and brought it to her midsection. "The midwife visited while you were on your ride, and we're fairly certain I am with child."

His mouth dropped open for a moment before he broke into a wide grin. After being so careful to ensure she wouldn't fall pregnant with their nightly activities before they'd wed, little had changed when they stopped being so careful. Month after month, she'd been disappointed when her courses arrived on time. At least all speculation about the haste of their marriage had been firmly put to rest.

He pulled her into an embrace, laughing. "How is it possible that I can be this fortunate?"

When he drew back to gaze down at her, a besotted smile on his face, she lifted one hand to rest along his smoothly shaven cheek. Their lives had already changed so much, and now they would change even more. Notoriety might await her when people learned she was the author of scandalous novels, but for now she had everything that she wanted with the man she loved.

Thank you for reading The Unexpected Marquess! I hope you love John and Amelia as much as I do. The next book in the Landing a Lord series tells Ashford and Mary's story. The Unwilling Viscount will be available in 2022.

And to learn about new books, sign up to my newsletter: https://www.suzannamedeiros.com/newsletter.

If you're looking for something short and sexy, check out Lady Hathaway's Proposal, the first book in my Hathaway Heirs series of novellas, which is FREE!

Turn the page to read a preview of Lady Hathaway's Proposal…

She will do anything for a few nights in his arms…

Twelve years have passed since Miranda Hathaway
ended her courtship with Andrew Osborne and
married the older, but much wealthier, Viscount
Hathaway. It is only one week after her husband's
death and Miranda cannot ignore the temptation to
have a taste of what she threw away all those years
ago when she followed her parents' wishes. But to
entice the man she never stopped loving, she will have
to act quickly.

Now the Earl of Sanderson, Andrew is no longer the
same man who once believed in love. When Miranda
asks him to help her conceive a child—one whom she
means to pass off as the next Hathaway heir—he sees
her deceit as proof that she is not the same woman he

once knew. However, he cannot ignore the temptation to finally have her in his bed.

Miranda knows she is infertile, but her deception gives her three weeks with Andrew. He plans to use that time to finally consign Miranda Hathaway to the past, while she hopes to build memories that will last her a lifetime.

UNTIL THAT MORNING the Earl of Sanderson would have said he was long past making a fool of himself for Miranda Hathaway, yet here he was, following her butler into the drawing room of her London town house. He told himself it was only curiosity that led him to accept her request for a meeting. After all, they hadn't seen one another in twelve years, so why on earth would she want to see him now?

He took in the room's ornate furnishings as the butler bowed and left to fetch his mistress. Viscount Hathaway had always made a point of displaying his vast wealth at every opportunity, as was evidenced by the amount of gilt in the room. He wondered if Miranda approved of the decor, or if she, too, found it lacking in taste. The old Miranda would have believed the latter. Or so he'd thought at the time, but that was before she'd broken it off with him to marry the much wealthier older man.

Unease settled in the pit of his stomach, and annoyed at the sign of weakness, he moved to the window and looked out onto the fashionable Mayfair neighborhood. It was early for a social call and the road was quiet. No doubt most of Miranda's neighbors were still abed, recovering from whatever entertainments had kept them up the evening before. He would have been sleeping as well if Miranda's message hadn't arrived last night before he'd left for his club.

He resisted the urge to turn around and leave, just as she had done that last time they'd seen one another. Once again, he was at a disadvantage with her. In her house, at her summons, no knowledge of what this meeting was about. He was not, however, the same untried youth he'd been back then. If Miranda assumed so, she would be more than a little surprised.

He sensed her approach and turned in time to see her enter the room. He couldn't help but notice she still moved with the same grace she'd possessed as a young woman, setting the ton ablaze during her first season with her beauty and unaffected charm. It had been inevitable that she'd captured his interest as well. But the new widow standing across the room from him now, clad in stark black, was far different from the girl of eighteen who'd worn only pale colors.

That was a lifetime ago.

"My lord," she said, executing a fluid curtsey. Her

expression gave no hint as to why she had sent for him.

He inclined his head in acknowledgement and watched in silence as she sat on one end of the ornate settee. A chair was positioned at an angle from her and it was clear she expected him to use it.

A need to ruffle her impassive bearing had him remaining silent and ignoring the chair. He moved past her and sat, instead, beside her on the settee. He left a respectable distance between them, but the way she stiffened told him she hadn't expected him to sit so close. It was self-indulgent, but he felt a small measure of triumph at her discomfort.

He watched, more than a little surprised, as she collected herself, smoothing away all signs of discomfort. Her body relaxed, her expression becoming one of polite cordiality as she held herself with an almost unnatural stillness. It appeared Miranda Hathaway had learned to control the youthful exuberance she'd once possessed. He wasn't sure whether to applaud her for her newfound reserve or mourn the loss of that once vibrant, impetuous young woman.

Silence stretched between them for several seconds before she turned to face him. He was struck once again, as he had been all those years ago, by her beauty. Her dark brown hair and the unrelieved black of her dress called attention to her pale coloring, making it seem as though she were carved from ivory. Her gray eyes were larger than he remembered, but she was also much thinner than when he'd known her. Almost painfully so. He almost asked if she was well but resisted the impulse. He had no desire to hear about how much she mourned the loss of the husband whose funeral had been only the week before.

The curve of her breasts and her unfashionably plump mouth were the only things about her that were still full. His eyes flickered downward and he remembered with unexpected vividness just how those full lips had felt under his. He'd been with many other women since they'd parted ways, but he'd never enjoyed kissing anyone as much as he had Miranda. Thoughts of how she could put that mouth to another use sent a wave of unwelcome heat through him.

He'd miscalculated. He'd wanted to set Miranda off balance, but being this close to her was having an unwanted effect on him.

"Thank you for accepting my invitation," she said, cutting through the uncomfortable silence. "I know it is early, but I can ring for tea if you haven't eaten yet this morning."

His wayward thoughts under control, he met her emotionless gaze with one of his own. "I think we can dispense with the niceties. We both know this isn't a social call."

Those luscious lips tilted ever so slightly at the corners. "I see you are still as direct as always."

"And I can see you've taken to hiding behind

social conventions. You were never one to dance around a subject. You asked me to visit and, despite my reservations, I came. You clearly have something you wish to discuss with me."

He was surprised when she stood.

"This was a mistake." She took a step toward the doorway. "Forgive me for inconveniencing you."

After a brief moment of hesitation, he rose from the settee and moved to block her path. She stopped but kept her eyes averted.

"Miranda."

She didn't move. Against his better judgment, he placed a hand under her chin and tilted her face up to his. They stood that way for several long moments, during which he was painfully aware of the small woman before him. The woman who, he now knew, still had the power to make him want her. She, on the other hand, had the appearance of a cornered, frightened animal.

He dropped his hand and kept his voice even, sensing she was a hairsbreadth away from bolting. "Why did you wish to see me?"

She hesitated and then he saw the resolve form in her eyes.

"Very well," she said before taking a step back.

She moved around him to the door, and this time he didn't stop her—he knew she wouldn't attempt to escape again. He expected her to ring for the tea she'd offered him and was taken aback when she closed the door and turned to face him again.

He raised an eyebrow in question but said nothing. She leaned back against the door for a moment before straightening and looking at him directly. Just as she used to do.

"You are aware my husband passed away last week."

"Yes," he said simply. "Please accept my condolences."

He should have offered them when she'd first come into the room, but after a nod of acknowledgment, she continued as though she hadn't noticed his breach in manners.

"The reason I asked you here has to do with his passing."

"Oh? I'll admit I have no idea why you'd want to see me."

Her smile was fleeting. "No, of course not."

She moved back to the settee and lowered herself onto it. This time when he followed, he didn't repeat his mistake of sitting next to her. But if she guessed at his reason for choosing the chair, she showed no sign of it.

"There is no delicate way to say this, so I must be blunt."

Her words, as well as her resolute manner, sent every one of his senses into high alert. He wasn't sure if she was aware she'd used those same words all those years ago when she'd told him she was marrying someone else. He was starting to regret preventing her from leaving the room.

"With my husband's nephew due to inherit the entirety of his estate, I will have to rely on his generosity in future."

Andrew had stayed as far away as possible from Hathaway—had tried not to think about him outside of those times he'd had to see him in the House of Lords—so he had no way of knowing if he'd ever met the man's heir.

"Given how important Hathaway's wealth was to you and your parents, surely you don't expect me to believe provisions for your future weren't made before your marriage."

She didn't react to the sarcasm in his tone. "I won't need to resort to begging in the street. But no one imagined I wouldn't provide my husband with an heir, so the settlement outlined for that eventuality is a small one." She hesitated and her eyes slid away from his before she continued. "I have spoken to our solicitor and he informs me that in cases where the widow is still of childbearing years, it is customary to wait a few months to ensure there is no heir on the way."

He couldn't stop his gaze from moving to her abdomen, but given the loose fit of her gown, it was impossible to see if it concealed a small bump. The wave of bitterness that rose at her words caught him off guard.

"I fail to see what this has to do with me."

He started to stand, but she reached across the small space that separated them and laid a hand on his knee. Her touch froze him to the spot and his awareness of the intimacy of their current situation intensified.

She moved back and clasped her hands sedately in her lap, but she hadn't been quick enough to keep him from seeing the telltale tremble in her fingers. "I am not with child," she said as though nothing of import had just happened, "but I am hoping that will not be the case for long."

His mind was still on the unwanted rush of desire her touch had elicited, and so it took him several seconds before he realized what she was suggesting. Air rushed out of his lungs as the full implication of her words hit him. Why she'd summoned him here so early when no one would be about in the street to see his arrival. Why she'd closed the door to make sure the servants wouldn't overhear their conversation.

He welcomed the anger that rose swiftly within him, but he refused to let her see it. He wouldn't give her the satisfaction of knowing she could command more than polite curiosity from him.

"I am afraid I still do not know what any of this has to do with me. I am sure your solicitor would be able to advise you much better than I."

A hint of frustration crossed her face before she masked it. Despite her attempt to appear detached and businesslike, the revealing expression told him she was more emotionally invested in their conversation than she wanted him to know.

"You were never one to be so obtuse, Andrew."

"You will excuse me, Lady Hathaway, if I ask for some of that bluntness you promised me."

Her control was slipping, for this time he clearly saw her wince when he'd used her title. The narrowing of her eyes was minute, but she hadn't been able to hide it. She didn't speak for several long moments, long enough for him to think he had won. He was surprised, therefore, when she straightened, drew back her shoulders and met his gaze squarely.

"I want to have a child and I would like you to be the father of that child."

Disbelief almost robbed him of words. When he opened his mouth to tell her exactly what he thought of her proposal, she continued, forestalling him.

"I am under no illusion that we can continue our former relationship. I will make no demands of you and no one will know the child is yours."

Disappointment tinged the anger burning within him as she spoke. The deceitful, conniving woman sitting before him now, the one who would blithely make plans to defraud the heir to her husband's estate of his rightful inheritance, bore no resemblance whatsoever to the woman he'd once known and loved.

And with that realization came the certainty that

he was well and truly free of the hold she had once held over him.

He started to refuse, but something held him back. He might no longer love Miranda, but he couldn't deny that he was still very attracted to her. And despite everything, this new woman sitting before him was a mystery he found himself longing to unravel.

"Can you have children? In twelve years you should have already had more than one."

She didn't hesitate before replying. "Robert was older. Our marriage was not a physical one."

He scoffed at that. "I hope you're not about to tell me you're a virgin."

She closed her eyes for a moment and it seemed as though his question had embarrassed her. Given her former bravado and what she had just asked of him, her reluctance to discuss the details surrounding her outrageous plan was more than a little out of place.

"No. In the beginning he visited me, but it was not long before he stopped."

"Why?"

Annoyance flashed across her face.

"How would I know why? I assumed he had a mistress, but I was not about to ask him."

He couldn't keep himself from asking the obvious question. "How long has it been?"

She looked back at him. "Long enough that I am certain I am not carrying his child."

Her answer was far from satisfactory, but since he

didn't want to hear the intimate details of her marriage, he didn't press her further.

They sat there for some time, holding each other's gaze, but neither one willing to make the next move. As the silence lengthened, his awareness of Miranda grew. Images of the two of them in bed, his hands sliding over every inch of her body, her face contorted in ecstasy as she found release, crowded his mind.

He didn't love Miranda, but he still wanted her. Perhaps he wanted to punish her as well. Give her a taste of all she had cast aside when she'd casually dismissed him for a larger fortune.

His lust for her wrestled with his conscience, but in the end it was his desire that won out, and he knew he would give her the affair she wanted. It would, of necessity, be of brief duration if she wanted to pass off his bastard as Hathaway's heir. And God help his black soul, but the thought gave him a sense of grim satisfaction. He'd have his revenge on Miranda, ruin her for any other man, and even the score with Hathaway for stealing the woman he'd so desperately wanted all those years ago.

If she wanted him to do this, however, she would have to work for it. She might have had everything she'd ever wanted fall neatly into her lap, but he was no longer willing to exert himself just because she crooked a finger in his direction.

"Satisfy my curiosity about something," he said, breaking the now oppressive silence. "Why me? I'm sure there are any number of men who would be willing to lie between your legs."

Her face heated at his deliberate crudeness, but he had to admire the fact that she didn't lose her composure.

"I know most men have no problem bedding whichever woman happens to be near at hand at the moment. I was young when I married, however, and have spent most of the last few years at our estate in Northampton. I never learned to be as casual as some women are about their bed partners. And…"

For a moment Andrew would have sworn she looked uncertain. Vulnerable. But clearly that could never be said about a woman who planned to pass off another man's child as the heir to a well-established title.

"And what?" he prompted when she showed no signs of continuing.

"You were once kind to me."

That was a vast understatement if ever he'd heard one. "Yes, well, kindness is the very last thing I feel for you now."

She said nothing to that. What was there to say?

"Did you want to start here or should we go up to your bedroom?"

That got a reaction. Her hand fluttered to her chest. "I'm not sure. Do you think it would be wise?"

She licked her lips, a gesture, he remembered, that always indicated she was nervous. His groin tightened.

He'd been trying to shock her, but it appeared she was quite willing to carry through with her proposition, and his body responded eagerly.

Irritated she could still so easily rouse his desire, he lashed out at her. "Tell me, Miranda, did Hathaway kiss you and caress you before fucking you? Or did he simply raise your nightgown and grunt away on top of you while you congratulated yourself on the excellent match you'd made?"

She didn't try to hide the anger his words had roused. Good, he thought. This was the Miranda he wanted. The calculating, aggressive Miranda. He wanted no reminders of how young and innocent she'd once been.

In reply, she stood. His innate manners had him beginning to stand, but she placed her hands on his shoulders to stop him. He leaned back in the chair and waited to see what she would do next. He wasn't disappointed.

She lowered herself onto his lap, leaned into him, and raised her hands to frame his face. He could feel the rapid rise and fall of her breasts against his chest and, in anticipation, his own breath quickened to match hers. She placed her mouth against his, and in that moment he wanted nothing more than to crush her against him and take what she so freely offered. Instead, he willed himself to remain still, letting her take the lead. She moved her mouth against his, but it soon became clear she'd acted out of bravado and not experience.

When she drew back again, frustration had etched little lines above her nose. Despite the fact she had given him little more than a chaste kiss, she was not unaffected. Her gray eyes had darkened and her breathing was ragged. Aside from confirming the type of marital relations she'd shared with her husband, her kiss had given him another piece of vital information. He needed more, and he needed it now.

When he stood, taking her with him, she gave a surprised gasp and wrapped her arms around his neck. He moved the two steps to the settee and lowered the two of them onto it. She remained on his lap, but now his arms were around her. Her eyes widened when she felt his erection pressing against her hip.

"Right, no kissing," he said, surprised to find his voice hoarse with his effort at controlling himself. "Let me show you how it's done."

He claimed her mouth slowly at first. Touching his lips to hers and brushing them against hers in slow, tantalizing movements aimed at gaining her trust. It was not too dissimilar from the way she had kissed him, but she obviously took comfort from the fact he was now participating. She relaxed against him and the heat of her body, pressed against his, fueled his desire.

He'd been all too innocent and eager to prove himself worthy of her when he'd courted her as a youth and so hadn't kissed her the way he'd longed to. But now, with the confidence that came from experience, he intended to make up for his former restraint. When she sighed, he took advantage of the opportunity to deepen the kiss, tracing his tongue first against her lips and then entering her mouth. She stiffened, but only for a moment before matching his movement.

The notion entered his mind that perhaps she'd been acting the innocent earlier, but he dismissed the notion as inconsequential. Did it really matter? He leaned back against the cushions and she followed, draping her body over his. He groaned as the kiss became more urgent, their tongues and mouths dueling for dominance. Blind to everything but the lust sweeping through him, he placed one hand on her backside and ground his erection against her hip. He lifted his other hand to cup her breast. She moaned low, arching into his touch as he covered her full breast and teased the hardened nipple with his thumb. She moved now, writhing against him. Without conscious thought, he shifted, reversing their positions so that she lay under him on the settee.

When he had her exactly where he wanted, he started to raise her skirts so he could settle between her legs. It took him a few moments to realize that her hands had moved from clinging to his shoulders to trying to push him away.

He lifted his head and looked down at her. Her lips were swollen from their heated kiss and a flush stained her cheeks and upper chest a rosy pink. She was clearly aroused. Behind the heat in her eyes, however, he detected a hint of uncertainty. Damn. How had he lost control so quickly? He closed his eyes, and took a deep breath before pushing himself away from her. He watched in silence as she struggled with her skirts before rising to sit on the other end of the settee. One hand moved to touch her bottom lip and he knew with certainty that neither her husband, nor any other man, had ever kissed her that way.

"Are you…" Flustered, she stopped before starting again. "Does this mean you agree to my request?"

Mere agreement was laughable when compared to the feelings warring within him. Desire. Lust. An almost desperate need to throw her back down and finish what they'd started. Oh yes, he would most definitely give her what she wanted. And at the same time he'd finally get Miranda Hathaway out of his system and be done with her. And if a child resulted… Well, he wouldn't be the first man with a bastard. And in his case he knew his son would be well provided for as the next Viscount Hathaway. And a daughter would also ensure Miranda had claims to the next Viscount's generosity.

Schooling his features to mask his anticipation, he rose and moved to the door. With one hand on the knob he turned back to face her.

"I'll send word of where and when."

At her nod he opened the door and, anxious to be away from Miranda and his newly aroused need for her, showed himself out.

Miss Hathaway's Wish

For more information please visit the author's website:
https://www.suzannamedeiros.com/books/

ABOUT SUZANNA

Suzanna Medeiros was born and raised in Toronto, Canada. Her love for the written word led her to pursue a degree in English Literature from the University of Toronto. She went on to earn a Bachelor of Education degree, but graduated at a time when no teaching jobs were available. After working at a number of interesting places, including a federal inquiry, a youth probation office, and the Office of the Fire Marshal of Ontario, she decided to pursue her first love—writing.

Suzanna is married to her own hero and is the proud mother of twin daughters. She is an avowed romantic who enjoys spending her days writing love stories.

She would like to thank her parents for showing her that love at first sight and happily ever after really do exist.

To learn about Suzanna's books, sign up for her newsletter:
https://www.suzannamedeiros.com/newsletter

Visit her website:
https://www.suzannamedeiros.com

Or visit her on Facebook:
https://www.facebook.com/AuthorSuzannaMedeiros

43074975R00200